AF425372

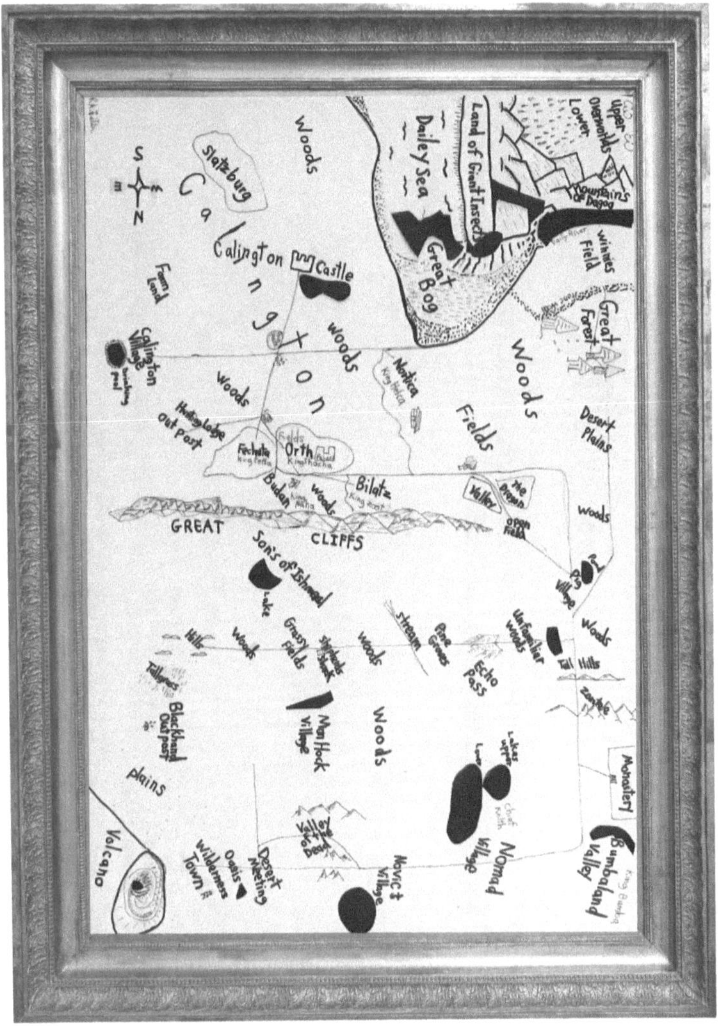

Upper Overworlds
Lower
Land of Giant Insects
Dailey Sea
Mountains of Dagog
Woods
S E N W
Slatzburg
Canyston
Calington Castle
Great Bog
Winnie's Field
Valley River
Great Forest
Farm Land
Calington Village
Woods
Nortica Kingdom
Woods
Fields
Desert Plains
Hustaslodge out Post
Fechata Kingdom
Fields Orth Kindthacha
Budan
Bilatz Kingdom
Woods
Valley
The Dream
Open Field
Woods
GREAT CLIFFS
Son's of Ishmael
Lake
Village
Hills
Woods
Greasy Fields
Shepherds Shack
Woods
stream
Pine Groves
Echo Pass
Unfamiliar woods
Tall Hills
Woods
Tall grass
Blackhand Out post
plains
Man Hock Village
Woods
Monastery
Volcano
Oasis Wilderness Town
Desert Meeting
Valley of the Beast
Novic Village
Nomad Village
Lukas upper Lake
Chief Keith
Bumbaland Valley
King Bumbg

Calington Castle X

"The Solution"

R. A. Feller

ISBN 979-8-9894920-9-1 (paperback)
ISBN 979-8-9894920-8-4 (eBook)

Printed in the United States of America

The Incident

Young Eagaldorf quietly examines animal tracks on the ground in the forest near his home. A bow and arrow are in his hand.

He suddenly catches the scent of a deer upon the wind and knows that it is close as he flairs his nostrils.

The teen hears the crack of some twigs on the ground. Placing an arrow softly to his bow, Eagaldorf raises them in the right direction.

He hears an arrow sing through the air and sees it kill his game before his eyes while on his own land.

He shouts at the rogue hunters, "Why are you hunting on my land?" He realizes they're wearing the uniforms of royal hunters.

One hunter dismounts from his horse and calls back, "You best mind your words as we are not poachers."

The other hunter looks up as he pulls the arrow from his kill and says, "Haven't you heard about the new edict from King Ronan?"

"No, I have not."

"All lands throughout the kingdom are now open for the royal hunters to hunt in."

"That's a lie!"

"You best mind your words, boy, as treason comes to mind."

The other hunter calls out while helping his partner mount the deer on the back of his horse, "Come over and we'll show you the mark on his decree."

Realizing he is outnumbered, Eagaldorf answers with a tone of suspicion while keeping his distance, "I'll take your word for it."

Putting away the scroll, the hunter continues to speak, "Good, lad! Why not come over and we'll cut you a leg for your trouble."

"Ahh, no thanks! I prefer the hunt more than the game anyway."

The two hunters look to themselves with a smirk as the other responds, "Suit yourself!"

A cabin door swings open and Eagaldorf enters with two rabbits in hand which he drops on the table before him. Rimka, his mother turns from a stove while acknowledging his entrance, "Praise God! You caught two rabbits, so why the glum face?"

He sits at the table next to a few peeled potatoes, a couple of sliced carrots, and some peeled quartered onions as he starts to go to work on skinning the game.

Rimka breaks the silence with a look while saying, "Well?"

Her son responds, "We almost had venison for a week."

"I cannot believe that anything could get away from you. You're such a good hunter, did something go wrong?"

"Yes, very wrong!"

"In the light of all the Lord has blessed us with, it can't be that bad. So, look up and never forget that our redemption draws nearer everyday. Now, what has you so uneasy?"

"Royal hunters were on our property today and poached a deer by royal decree while I was hunting. They snatched my hunt with an arrow of their own when I was about to shoot."

"There must be some kind of mistake, for King Ronan would never go back on his word."

"That's what I said. I even called them liars."

His mother says with concern, "Did they mention treason?"

"How did you know?"

"I suspect that they were lying, too."

Ronan continues, "But why would they do this?"

"I mustn't be too quick to tend to my tongue, they might not know that something is amiss and are just following out orders."

"But from who?"

Rimka takes a large pot filled with water and places it on the table, "It looks like you're about finished with those rabbits," she next starts placing the vegetables in the water.

"From who, mother?"

She takes the skinned rabbits and puts them in the pot and says, "Would you be kind enough to place our dinner on the stove? I am rather hungry."

"Very well." Rising from the table, he carries the stew over and places it on the hot stove.

"Eagaldorf, you know that we do not wrestle against flesh and blood, but spiritual wickedness in the high places, don't you?"

"Is that all you have to say?"

"Have faith in the Great One and all will work out."

"You and your faith. Always praying …"

"… And what's wrong with that?"

"I feel it is time to take action while there is yet time. Perhaps some of our neighbors are experiencing a similar situation."

Rimka sits at the table after placing a few more large sticks in the fire within the stove and folds her hands in silent prayer. A few moments later, Eagaldorf spies his mother who opens her eyes and catches his mother's glance. "Come son, sit with me. You know that it is always best to pray before taking any action."

He sits and looks her in the eyes, "One day, I might not agree with you, mother. For, I feel a time of action might soon be at hand."

"What do the ten commandments say?"

"You're not going to pull 'Honor your mother and father' on me again."

"I just did, and knowing that He put us here as God's love constrains us, His love continues to hold as you know that I love you."

" You're right, mother. Thank you for your words of wisdom as my patience was about at its end."

A knock is heard at the door and Rimka calls from the table, "Whether you be friend or foe, you're welcome to come in and pray with me and my son as we're about to address The Lord of heaven and earth."

The door slowly opens and some neighbors appear standing in the doorway. "Come in, one and all, as this seems like divine timing."

A group of men, five in all, silently enter the cabin. Rimka takes notice of their faceless expressions while recognizing them, "Before you state your business, prayer is in order."

Sage enters first, followed by trig, Honer, Seth, and finally, Benjah. All seek the wisdom of Eagaldorf's mother, Rimka, for answers. They quietly sit at the table and attentively open their ears to hear her prayer.

"Oh, Great One, hear the cries of our heart for vindication as something has happened within our kingdom that seems unjust at present. Keep us at peace in your presence so that we do not lose the perspective of focusing on You with full trust, Amen."

All around the table respond with hardy amen's of their own as well. The men look to each other before Sage who volunteers to share what needs be said to the others, which has brought them to the table at present. "Rimka, it was around noon when I saw it happen to Sailo. I was out hunting when I heard a commotion off in the distance and saw our fellow woodsmen being wrestled to the ground by some royal hunters. After he was secured, they placed a rope around his neck and led him away with his hands tied behind his back. Poor Sailo, they were so ruff. I feel in my guts that he won't be seen again."

Eagaldorf interrupts, "Then I was right not to go to the hunters when they invited to share their kill on our land!"

Sage responds, "They must have enticed him in the same way as the hunters had fresh game with them as well."

Trig becomes involved, "They're after our lands I tell you!"

Honer shouts, "King Ronan has all he needs. It just doth not seem to add up."

Seth suggests, "Perhaps we could band together?"

Benjah interjects, "… And who would lead us?"

Rimka breaks in on what is about to be an argument, "Gentleman, please!"

Heads turn to Rimka and all become silent when turning to her.

Eagaldorf responds, "My mother is very wise."

The men say agreeingly, "Then it is settled."

Rimka stiffens her lips before speaking, "How soon you forget our Lord who is wiser than us all. Let us agree to seek His wisdom and I will lead in prayer."

All the men say together, "It is agreed."

Rimka bows her head, "Good Lord. You have said in your word that if we are lacking in wisdom, ask unwaveringly in our faith and you shall grant it." Sage answers after looking at all, "Everyone is in agreement and acknowledges your word, amen."

Eagaldorf sits up and proclaims, "A thought just came to me. Why not seek counsel from King Liam, the deliverer?"

Rimka asks, "Are there any disagreements with my son's suggestion?" There is silence in the room. "Then it is decided, this is what we shall do."

Trig makes the statement, "Who shall go among us?"

Rimka speaks again, "The Spirit spoke through my son, Eagaldorf. So, he is the one to go."

Honer volunteers, "You can use my horse as it is the swiftest in all of Eridu."

Benjah gets involved, "Nay! It is not a good idea. For if he was seen, it might arouse suspicions in the light of what is happening."

Rimka says, "That is the voice from the Spirit of God's wisdom."

Seth responds, "But nobody would be able to catch him."

Sage interacts as well, "An arrow could take him down pretty easily. Nothing should appear out of the ordinary that might upset our progress. If things were suddenly speeded up, it might not give us a chance to retaliate if anything were to go wrong."

Rimka speaks out, "He shall take his own horse and all will come to pass in our Lord's timing. This house shall be our meeting place. You are all to return to your homes and not say anything to anyone about what might be happening. For if word got out, retaliation could be swift. However, you will casually load your wagons with supplies and if you're noticed, you shall say we will be going on a trip. Any further questions about a destination, you shall answer, "I've been called of the Lord and know not where I'm going yet."

"All is understood," is heard among the men in response to her instructions.

Rimka continues, "Sage, you manage the most land and have many men in your service, beware of spies who might have relatives at court among you from inner Eridu. If you manage to conceal your actions well, there might be an even greater task for you. This I must pray about. Trig, you are the smallest land owner, so it shall be easier for you to get around without arousing suspicion. You shall be our scout. Honer, I want you to pay the Monsignor a visit at the monastery in Ostrog. Inform him of what is going on as prayer support will be needed. Perhaps we can avoid a war if God's conscience is awakened to push back the darkness of what is going on."

Honer adds, Yes! It is time the torch be lit as The Great One's light must illuminate the mind's of all men once again."

Seth and Benjah look to Rimka anticipating instruction for them as well. After hearing nothing further, silence falls upon all of them again. Finally

Rimka speaks once more, "Seth, would you do me a service and remain with me until my sun returns?"

"The servants can tend to my wife's needs. I'll look after you while your son is away, but should he tarry for longer than a week, perhaps Benjah could relieve me.

"Those were my exact sentiments, that is if it's okay with you, Benjah?"

"Agreed."

"Well, gentlemen, seeing how we are all in one accord, let it be Known that God's Spirit is with us. So, the time to act must be now. On the morrow at 3pm, the hour of our Lord, all shall go into effect. In this way we'll have time to settle our affairs before setting out and our conscience will be clear."

The Conversation

$\mathcal{A}$ voice is heard in the dark from a realm at the bottom of the trough in the motions of time. Something is hiding in the recesses of darkness which says, "Lexum, I have received word from The Supreme Creator. Once again, you are to be sent on a mission above to bring down another soul to be our prize. We have much to gain from this one as his mother is a prayer warrior who petitions the Creator all the time for him. Because all her heart is in it everyday, his soul will be a very valuable one."

"Master, what is the victim's name so that I may find him through the words of others more readily?"

"His name is Eagledorf and just so they'll be no mistake, he dwells with his mother, Rimka, in the forests of Eridu."

"Wait Master! If his mother prays for him and he is a man of faith, how then am I to gain access into Eagledorf's soul?"

"That is for you to find out. Though, word has it that he is troubled because of recent circumstances of food becoming scarce. I know that deep down inside, he struggles between his father's accidental death and trusting that The Supreme Creator is truly trustworthy when it comes to being with Him. You must keep him focused on thoughts that lead him away from what The High King has to offer or he will become a great enemy against us. Now because his mother is very rich in faith, if you succeed in leading him to join our fiery kingdom, his mother may curse The Supreme One and join him. We are preparing her to blame herself by keeping her rough around the edges as a poor example before her son. She'll feel she could have been a better example to him and I have an agent working on her through a relative to keep her a poor one. When the time comes, her guilt will drive her mad."

"What is my role?"

"Lexure, later today something is going to happen to Eagledorf in the realm of the breadth of time and he may decide to enter pride where he'll renounce his faith by believing in lies. You must find him before he does this and intervene. For should he choose the darkness of his own wisdom by pride over light, you shall have a bridge to enter his soul. So make our darkness seem like it is brighter than The Great One's brilliance shall ever be."

"How did the boy's father die and what is the circumstance that he shall find himself in?"

"The boy's father was killed in a hunting accident and he shall be reminded of his anger towards God when he meets King Liam on the main road between Eridu and Calington Castle. When his anger rises within, this will be the time to lay darkness in. We will await his decision and see if he prefers the power of his anger over love within his pride to enter him into the door of our kingdom. Once inside, Eagaldorf shall soon forget the purpose of his life as his brilliance will grow dim 'til preferring what is in the scent of darkness over light.

"This will not be an easy task as you have said that his mother always prays."

"You have a point, Lexure. Perhaps an agent can be sent by way of a relative as a distraction to her, for our cause."

A Great Boar

King Liam looks to his son, "Seems like just yesterday you became crowned, King Ronan of Eridu, and now that you've been confirmed into the church by receiving baptism of the Holy Spirit, what a glorious day this is!"

Ronan is all smiles when his father gives him a serious look, causing him to question, "What is it?"

"The Lord shall give you wisdom even beyond all those who have been advising you. So, be cautious to listen with understanding as attitudes can be difficult to discern when people are speaking. Any distancing or uneasiness of speech could mean that someone is trying to protect what is pleasing to them in the dark as hidden areas in someone's character can mask over a secret life. A wink or a quiver of smile which distracts from genuineness must be noted. For when a soul is stirred to be shaken within while in conversation, a deception can be in the making. Yet, be patient. Do not accuse as nothing will be kept back when walking in God's light. Remember to take notes and be sure to present them when delivering facts."

"What causes you to tell me this?"

"Beware of prolonged silence when among those who you perceive as friends and always remain teachable, never believe to know it all as pride always shall come before a great fall. Now in answer to your question as to why I speak of what I speak, it is sensed that my time here on earth might be nearing its end."

"Then let us pray, father, that this doth not happen."

"We will pray, but remember it rains on the just and the unjust."

"How can you tell that God is going to take you home with such certainty?"

"I had a dream about being attacked by a wild animal and that one of my old servants who was caught as a thief came upon me, yet did nothing to help me."

"Perhaps if you remain aware, you'll be able to avoid what you sense is going to happen by asking God in prayer."

"Your wisdom bears witness with the truth I know. Yet whether I live or die our Lord shall continue to be my source of joy. For whatever is going to happen will happen if it is my time. So, my attitude must not waiver as always blessed is the name of The Lord while facing any adversity of fear. Do not be robbed from the brilliance of knowing Him, too. Straight way, I suggest you be honest about what you feel, for when not joined to the truth, darkness can always claim you as its prize."

"Father, did you understand the full meaning of your dream?"

"A beast of some kind, either spiritual or physically will attack me, this I am certain of, and the second part of the dream has to do with people not getting involved. They are like thieves that feed off of others' labor as their inactiveness causes a rippling effect that has an effect on the rest of the tribe. I have concerns about our kingdom family remaining unified, for we can lose our value when monetary gain is involved. Know it now, Ronan, greed is a spirit that lacks heart as it doth not know love."

"So, you're saying that people who are lacking in connections of affection and seek only money shortchange themselves? Hmmm! Distractions of coin can cause them to miss the point of God's focus on love."

"Even more than that, for love is a spirit which draws every man to give more than what they have for the sake of it."

"Why is that?"

"For seeing yourself in another, a heart is stirred to compassion and with this kind of attitude, heaven is quick to become your reward."

"I see now. God repays all who trust Him for their kindness as they truly are His citizens when love is in the atmosphere."

"This is a part of walking in the light, Ronan. For when nothing holds you back, you are free in spirit and in truth to know the differences between being bound and loosed."

"Then a part of discernment is being able to tell the differences between those who love much and love little as this truly tells what kingdom they are from."

"Wisdom is a part of this picture, too. You'll be able to tell a tree by the fruit that it bears as forgiveness is a part of the picture of love. Beware of those who make resentful faces and carry a grudge. For there is a darkness that hides other spirits that lack affection which are from beneath and above which do not harbor love. They choose to dwell in the underworld rather than a light that bears the warmth of affection …"

"… From what you say, there are certain people in Eridu who come to mind."

"Then be alerted, for a kingdom divided against itself will not stand."

"What then should I do, father, as I have seen many hardened hearts as of late."

"Are you just as in touch with all your people as before?"

"Only by the reports I receive from my advisors."

"How would you discern the characters of those who are giving you your reports as of late?"

"Rather ambitious in the way they aim to please."

"Ronan, what I am going to tell you next is very important."

"Say on."

"Do you make eye contact with all the people you talk to?"

"For the most part, yes."

"What do you mean by, for the most part?"

"Well, sometimes when talking they seem to lose interest and look away. Though, they still listen 'til I'm finished."

"This can mean one of two things. You are either giving them more information than they can handle at that moment or they discount you as king, perhaps having an alternative to your rule in their mind."

"Oh, I have played the fool! For the second thing you have described weighs heavily upon my mind."

"It sounds as though you have become too comfortable in your position of rule and complacency has set in."

"What would you recommend I do?"

"To avoid this in the future, you must always remember to make and keep eye contact with people when speaking with them. Try to be a better listener than talker, for if someone feels that they are not getting their needs met, after a season they won't remain loyal to listen but tune out your voice and that of your kingdom."

"I have been feeling rather alone lately, father."

"This could be more serious than I had first thought."

"What do you mean?"

"Who are your closest advisors right now?"

"There is a business owner who manages his affairs well that has gained my ear named Gunta, who seems to get along with all my associates rather well."

"What about Pine, Cunna, and Gray? What have they been telling you lately?"

Gray is away on vacation for a season. Gunta, the advisor, recommended it, for he has been working so hard. Pine is involved with many litigations at court as magistrate and since the palace has been completed, Cunna has gotten involved with becoming a missionary. He takes priests to foreign lands to spread the word of The Great One while I have been attending to the affairs here. You seem to have come at a divine time, father."

"It doth appear that way and this is what I recommend you do as your life may be in danger."

"Aren't you being a little too caring?"

"If you do not want to hear what I have to say, then I will go."

"I'm sorry. Speak your mind, father."

"With many of your advisors away, the peoples confidence may be weakened and this would be a good time for a revolt."

"Say on!"

"Good, you're getting to be a better listener already. Now I shall speak. There is a certain woman called Rimka, who has a son named Eagaldorf. They live deep within the forest of Eridu. You shall go to them as a traveler who doth odd jobs. You've been trained to know all skills of trade while running the kingdom, have you not?"

"…And my hands are just as crafted as my skills are, for I have just finished the challenge of building my own coach."

"Perfect!"

"What do you mean by perfect?"

"You shall leave the palace and live among the people and find out what their opinion is of you. If their opinion of you is bad then you will know that there is trouble in the administration of those who now are your advisors. From the outside, you will be able to learn who you can and cannot trust."

"But what if the people have a bad opinion of me?"

"You must allow them to learn of your character, then once you have gained their confidence, reveal to them who you truly are."

"Wait a minute! How shall I slip out of the palace or even prove who I am to get back in once I am out?"

"I have a plan."

In a dimly lit room, without windows, a secret meeting begins when the last of the men enter. A hand goes up to quiet the men as the last of the group of ten joins them, "Settle down now!" Gunta calls out. "When the men become silent he continues, "We all know why we're here." In response all eyes of the other nine turn towards him, "King Liam has arrived in our province and now that preparations have been made, especially with Cunna away, it is time to implement our plan."

Link, one of the more aggressive one's, speaks out, "Pine, betrayed us. It is against our nature not to war."

Papps, another from the group agrees, "King Liam should have been courteous enough to make sure that we got paid for our service as jurors to pine."

"Swan becomes involved as well, King Ronan doth not suspect that we are undermining his authority, soon the land owners will want him dead."

Thortan, joins the conversation, "Years of planning are finally beginning to pay off, soon Eridu will be ours."

Wilaxe speaks his mind, "The dark lord from the underworld, shall have a harvest by the energy that was created from all the joy."

Dunge, gets enthused, "Now that we are strong everyone will be taken by surprise!"

Gunta comments, "The boarlet's blood has been painted on the belly of King Liam's horse." Looking to the last man who entered the room, "Isn't that right, Gordy."

Gordy answers, "… And I threw some dirt over it that no one would notice. Freedom shall reign for the warrior's again at King Ronan's fall."

Gunta laughs, "Just as long as mother boar notices the scent of her baby upon it." The rest of the men join in and laugh as well as he looks to the man in the group who is larger than anyone else, "Remember, Scorch, it must appear to be an unfortunate turn of events for King Liam. In this way, it will keep them guessing if he was out of favor with God or not and by the time they figure it out, Eridu will be ours."

Scorch replies, "He never should have chastised me for helping myself to what was rightfully mine, all of you know I rightly deserved extra for all the work I did. I hope he suffers greatly in payment for what he did to me."

Gunta stands up to his size as he comments, "Just see to it that all works to our advantage."

"Don't worry, from what I know of their precious Calington kingdom, by the time Prince Edward comes around to wearing the crown, a new and bloody time will once again be where a true warrior rules by might!"

Sekco, feeling left out, joins in the camaraderie, "We shall pillage again!"

Having mounted his horse, King Liam looks to Ronan who stands dressed in his royal garb with a large filled gunny sack over his shoulder, "You know what to do now, son. Remember to be mindful, a true warrior knows how to maintain his composure while looking to the Lord. For He will always send help to those who guard their hearts while facing adversity before Him. Hold to His love and go in this confidence, never look back as the Lord is with us even to the end of the age."

King Liam and Ronan part ways, his son takes steps in one direction while he rides up the main drag in another. The Calington King shouts while facing forward, "Remember, never look back!"

Ronan tearfully turns his head with a new focus and starts on his way.

A rock is dropped by Gordy as a signal for Scorch to wait three minutes. He stands on a large crate wedged in the mouth of the rocky crag containing a mother boar of over 200 lbs. that frantically squeals for her boarlet. He then makes ready on the rope to open the top of the holding pen and use it as a shield to prevent possible retaliation.

Coming off of Trung Road from out of Eridu, which was once the Northern forests of Nortica, King Liam finds himself on the main thoroughfare heading towards Calington Castle. Reminiscing about some earlier crusades, he is found joyous of having been blessed throughout his years. King Liam then feels a large breath rise up within him and exhales in gratitude to the Lord for having given him a full life.

All at once, he hears a thrashing sound coming through the woods as he nears the turn off to the grotto to pass by what used to be called the "Valley of the Dragon."

The side of the horse is seen by the approaching mother boar. At the last second, Liam flinches to turn his head but does not. The animal's underbelly is ripped open by the incensed mother and as it collapses, the sow's tusks follow through ripping into the king as well. The distraught boar then keeps going on a blood covered run deep into the woods.

Scorch calls to Gordy, "Tend to the crate, I'm going over to have a look."

Gordy argues, "It's a bit much for me alone."

"Use your horse with a rope and make sure you dispose of it well."

Scorch approaches a dying King Liam who recognizes him as he lay bleeding to death, "If you don't help me many will die."

"That's a good thought, along with … how sweet is revenge."

"Wait! I want you to see that I am at peace."

Scorch is standing with a stare on his face when Gordy approaches on his horse. The crate is on a little wagon that he pulls. "Why are you standing here? Go get your horse and let's get out of here."

Gordy takes off up the main road and soon after Scorch catches up to him. They ride up the road a ways together 'til Gordy asks, "What did you see as you stayed there a long time?"

"Just a man die … and I am reminded that he shall be the first of many."

"All in good time as the Magistrate is not yet ours."

Arrivals

A three o'clock sun hangs in the late afternoon sky, signaling the timing for all to act. Movements both for and against oppression in the Land of Eridu are now coming to fruition.

Honer saddles his horse and starts for the Monastery as Trig starts to ride around and scout for possible trouble in the woodland's of Eridu.

After kissing his mother on the cheek, Eagaldorf mounts his horse and makes for the road as well. As he approaches the main road, He comes upon a young traveler with a hooded robe carrying a gunny sack. It is King Ronan in disguise and he is about the same age as the teen who discovers him while on his horse. Becoming intrigued and slowing to a pause, Egaldorf enquires, "Who might you be?"

"My name is Scott."

"Aren't you a bit young to be out here on your own?"

"Not so, I am a craftsman and able to earn my way for a price."

"Can you make a crossbow?"

"I've tools in my sac, I don't see why not."

"Up the road, at the third turn-off, if you take that trail you will come to a small wooden cabin in about three miles. Knock on the door and tell Rimka that Eagaldorf has hired you to make five cross-bows. We shall talk on my return."

"Don't you want to at least see my workman-ship with one before making five?"

"You look like you have an honest face." He then rides on leaving Ronan who continues on his way.

Thanking the Lord for showing him favor, He then starts to sing unto the Lord while continuing on his way to the castle.

"You are more than wonderful … and full of glory, and full of glory, and full of glor-or-ryyy!

You are more than wonderful … and full of glory, and full of glory is your name!

You have broken down the walls and set the captives free

You are more than wonderful, more than wonderful!

You have broken down the walls and set the captives free

You are more than wonderful, more than wonderful!

You are more than wonderful … and full of glory, and full of glory, and full of glor-or-ryyy! and full of glory is your name!"

At the same time, there is something else going on in the woods. Trig smells some smoke off in the distance and without being seen, he further investigates.

A group of several hunters are reclining around an open fire cooking game for themselves. A large deer roasts on a spit hung over two large Y-branches on either side. Trig, upon hearing voices, dismounts his horse after leading it out of sight. He quietly makes his way through the woods until being able to hear what they're saying.

Eagaldorf has just turned off of Trung road and starts to make his way towards Calington Castle. All at once he starts to get a sharp pain in his gut which causes him to ride a little faster. He next hears some loud grunting sounds from up the road and when he looks further on, a great boar is noticed feasting on the remains of a dead body and horse carcass. It has eaten so much of them that it is hard to differentiate between the two. Eagaldorf is quick to draw an arrow and when he slows his horse for a shot, the beast becomes alerted and starts to charge at him. He calls to his horse, "Steady Bucky." The horse doth not move and when his shot is certain, the arrow sings out piercing the boar's head through its eye which pins the beasts head to its leg, causing it to squeal outloud as it hobbles to the ground. A second arrow is loaded and this time the shot through the heart which silences the beast.

Eagaldorf dismounts and pulls a long knife out of his saddle bag and proceeds to cut off its head for a bounty. Boars, being very dangerous, have a good price on their head. Each one fetching a two week wage, which is a tidy sum. An inner voice that he has not heard before, tells him to tend to where the beast was feeding. A glimmer of light catches the sun's rays and as Eagaldorf gets closer, he realizes that he is staring at King Liam's crown.

Lexure, a demon from the underworld is standing next to Eagaldorf, but is unseen by him. He whispers into his ear, *"Your father died the same way!"* The pain in his gut becomes more intense as he hears the strange inner voice once again, *"God still remains against you, so forget about your mission and feast on the boar that's been killed, you've earned it. Remember how your father suffered as he slowly bled to death. You'll feel better after a good meal. Have you forgotten the taste of fresh pork?"*

He next hears another inner voice sounding like the voice of his praying mother, *"In all circumstances, hold faith as a shield to quench all flaming arrows of the evil one. Guard your heart and mind so that the peace of God, which surpasses all under-standing, will hold you steadfast in the times of temptation."*

A knock is heard on the cabin door and Rimka's mind becomes diverted from prayer, "Who's there?"

"It's your sister, Louisa!"

"Louisa? You came all the way from the village of Blackhand. What brings you here?"

"Well, aren't you going to let me in? I have an armful of gifts for you, Rimka."

Rising up, she goes over and opens the door and sees her sister standing there with two baby goats, one under each arm. "They're beautiful! Oh! Come in. It is good to see you, Louisa. You must be tired after such a trip, come and sit." She looks out the door. "Is there anyone with you?" She sees her husband Eztree outside in the wagon passing down some sacks of grain to Seth.

Back on the road to Calington Castle, Lexure continues to taunt young Eagaldorf, *"Succulent meat off the bone, how good and sweet, remember!"*

"Father first, and now King Liam." Eagaldorf suddenly vomits, then speaks out in a prideful angry tone while making a vow, "I shall never have roasted boar again!" At once, the demon disappears while entering into his mind through an ear. It begins to ring in his thoughts within a low tone. Holding his hand up to his ear, he cries out in anguish, "Ahhg!"

The crown catches his eye and the inner voice catches his attention again, *"Melt down the crown and coin the gold, no one would be the wiser."*

"No, His family has the right to know what has happened to our beloved King."

"Do they ... "

Louisa shares her concerns about Rimka's situation, "Are there any marriage prospects as of yet?"

"No, why do you ask?"

"Then who's the man outside that met us?"

"A neighbor. Just a kind friend who volunteered to look in on me while Eagaldorf is on errand."

"It has been two years since your husband died on the hunt. Eagaldorf would have an easier way of life if he had help from a new husband."

"God is my husband … and hard work helps build character. My boy is learning. He now looks to the Lord for provision and my prayers help to guide him towards wisdom."

"But is that enough?"

"Why don't you ask him? For he is a man and capable of making decisions by himself now."

"How can you tell?"

"I watch him look to the Lord and he doth what is right by Him."

"Where is he now?"

"Knock! Knock! Knock!" Is heard at the door.

"It looks like that answer will have to wait." Rimka goes to the door and asks, "Who's there?"

"My name is Scott. Your son, Egaldorf, commissioned me to build him some crossbows."

She opens the door and questions Scott while looking upon Him sack and all, "Eagaldorf is on errand. How is it that he acquired your services?"

"We met on the thoroughfare. You must be Rimka."

"Well, Scott, You can set up shop in the barn."

"Thank you, ma'am." She closes the door as he starts on his way.

Louisa comments, "Crossbows? What would you need them for?"

Another knock is heard on the door?

She turns and questions, "Did you forget something, Scott?"

"It's Trig, can I come in?"

Her sister comments again, "I thought it be more quiet out here in the woods."

"I'll explain later … Come in, Trig."

He enters while speaking what's on his mind, "I just found out that not all the royal hunters are royal hunters. The ones in charge were outsiders because I didn't recognize their names." He then notices Louisa as he regains his breadth.

Rimka sees his look and quickly sizes up the situation, "It is okay to talk, she's family."

Louisa asks, "What's going on here, Rimka?"

"What I'm going to say is not to leave this room, for if word got out, it would mean the lives of us all."

Rimka suggests, "I believe it best that we call in the others and have a meeting."

"Who was the lad I saw walking from the door?"

"He is someone my son hired to build us crossbows."

"Hmmm! Could be a spy."

"Would a spy be building crossbows to use on his own people?"

"I don't know, Rimka. I just don't know."

Outside the house, Seth and Eztree continue to unload the wagon, "You bringing these supplies with your wife is a most welcome gift as we've had problems with royal hunters poaching our game."

Eztree responds, "I thought King Ronan was fair with his people, something seems amiss."

Seth agrees, "It doth not sit right with me either."

"On our return to the village, I shall bring this up before our council. I shall not have my sister-in-law worry as she is apart of our tribe and will not stand alone."

In the barn, King Ronan Scott Calington, turns his head from his work after overhearing their conversation, *"So, it's true my inner circle of advisors have not been honest with me, but for what purpose?"*

He next overhears more from within the barn as Trig announces, "Come in the house, gents, we're going to have a meeting."

Scott continues pondering to himself, *"If I keep out of sight, I will be safe. Yet who would run the kingdom and would my reputation be even further tarnished before my people to do me further harm? Could the weapons that I am building for them be as my own gallos?"*

Looking down, he drops the crossbow from his hands that was starting to take shape. He then slowly picks it up and continues to work, *"What other choice do I have? I know, perhaps when Rimka's guests leave, I can catch a ride with them?"*

From Calington Onward

On the morn of the next day, Eagaldorf stands at Calington Castle Court with his head bowed, being apprehensive about what he will tell Prince Edward. Receiving coin for the boar's head was a less than cheerful event for him, even though the money shall be a great help for him and his mother. The sheriff even commented while paying him, "Hey, you should be glad that it was the boar's funeral and not yours." Finally, a guard bids him entrance to stand before the prince who is handling all affairs while his brother King Liam is away.

Walking slowly, the youth discreetly carries a sack. Then losing his composure, he just stands and stares before Prince Edward.

The prince questions, "What is it lad?"

Eagaldorf starts to sob and as he raises the bag to open it, he manages to get the words out, "I loved him, too." The sack slips and when he catches the corner at the bottom of it, King Liam's bloody crown rolls out on the floor. Him dropping to his knees, sobbing, sets the tone for everyone else in the room.

Silent tears roll down his brother's face who decrees, "Lower the flags half way, for we are in morning." He looks to Eagaldorf and inquires, "How did it happen?"

"I was on my way to seek his guidance about poachers belonging to the royal hunters from Eridu when I came across a boar eating ... eating a rider and his horse dressed in royal clothes. Then I came upon the crown."

"I take it by the pouch you bear that the boar is dead."

"Yes, my Lord."

"Royal hunters poaching doth not sound right, there shall be investigations of both my brother's death and your situation. Perhaps they are connected in some way. For a boar on the main road sounds suspicious to me. Send for Sergeant James," he calls to the messenger.

Later on, Eagaldorf rides with Sergeant James as they come upon some vultures which they shoo away from the corpse upon arrival. Sergeant James is quick to dismount from his horse and starts his investigation as his riding companion excuses himself, "I must be getting back to my mother or she will begin to worry."

"I might need to ask further questions of you. What is your location in the woods of Eridu?"

"We are off the main thoroughfare in the North West quadrant. There are several turns into the woods on either side, me and my mother, Remka, live off of the fifth turn to the right in a large cabin with a barn, we are about three miles in."

"On second thought, I will be coming out. For I still have to look into the royal hunters' poaching of game."

"I can arrange a meeting at eve in our cabin in anticipation of your arrival if you like?"

"That would be fine and this way I can give a full report to Prince Edward sooner than later. Best be on your way as I'm sure you'll be making stops to invite others for the meeting before you make it home."

"See you back at the house, Sergeant." At that, Eagaldorf turns and kicks his horse and starts on his way. James then turns his head and notices two large footprints in the dirt half covered in dried blood. He next sees a break in the bushes from where the boar thrashed its way through and tracks its footprints to the mouth of what used to be "The Valley of the dragon," but is now, "Prince Liam's Pass." The tracks stop at its opening. On further investigation, he notices relatively fresh wagon tracks and crate impressions within the opening of the pass. The Sergeant even spies an unusual stone which seems a little small to have fallen from the top on its own, *"Yes. A signal!"*

Honer is on horse taking the turn which leads to the monastery. When he is bid entrance, it is stated to the keeper at the gate that he is there on urgent business, concerning the woodland owners of Eridu. Inside while passing through the floral garden by the main entrance, taken in by all the different colors and fragrances, a childlike fascination overtakes him. Once inside, he is now curious as to what else there is to discover. Soon after being led through many corridors with picturesque paintings and drapery adorning the windows, a few more twists and turns lead him up a flight of stairs where they come to a stop before two hand carved wooden oak doors.

Honer inquires of his guide, "I'm sorry, I did not quite get your name. With all the wonder in this place, I guess I got distracted."

"My name is Jerome and many who come the first time react the same way as you."

"It must take quite a lot of time and hard work to keep a place of this size."

"At first, it seemed that way. Though after quite a few lessons, we learned that we can do all things through Christ who strengthens us. Then everything disappeared in comparison to his beauty."

"Quite interesting, my name is Honer," he extends his hand in friendship and Jerome takes it.

"Come, let us see if the monsignor is receiving visitors or if he has something pressing at hand.

Jerome knocks with Honer by his side.

Bartholomew, the new monsignor, calls out, "Who is there?

"Jerome! I have Honer here with me representing the voice of the woodsmen of Eridu."

"How is it that you decided to come to us?"

"After holding a meeting at Rimka's and the mother of Eagaldorf's house, it was determined that one be sent to seek counsel. I, Honer, am that one."

"You may come in."

Inside the office, a feast of paintings and ornate books upon cases carved into the walls capture his eyes. The Monsignor sees his mindfulness as his vision next beholds the rich intricacies on the framework of his cherrywood desk.

"It's amazing how easy it is to become distracted with what may appear to be the finer things in life. For every blessing is a gift to enhance our relationship with the giver of it or a curse should we neglect to thank our maker in each momentous task. My name is Monsignor Bartholomew and I take it you are Honer from Jerome's announcement at the door."

"Yes, your Eminence."

"I hear that you have a message from the woodsmen of Eridu."

"Royal hunters have been poaching from our lands and we fear approaching King Ronan without the support of the church could turn out badly."

"Sounds like Rimka has given you good counsel. Has word been sent to King Liam as well?"

"Her son, Eagaldorf, has undertaken that task."

"Very good! Jerome, could you find Father Marcus and coax him in for a visit?"

"I'm on the way."

"Oh!" Jerome stops and turns his head with an alert look. "Bring Father Jim, too. After summoning Marcus, leave him be as he shall arrive in the Lord's timing."

"Yes, your Eminence."

Honer expresses himself, "I'm sure glad we have your ear as they'll not be expecting representatives from the church in their midsts to settle things."

He sits looking on as the Monsignor states, "God works in mysterious ways."

"How so?"

"Father Jim has become rather ambitious in his organizing and has forgotten how to love the common people whereas Father Marcus has immersed himself in his reading as of late and lost sight of just how gracious God is with sinners who are finding their way …"

"… So you feel if you put the two of them together in this situation, it would bring each of them to a place of more effectiveness? I never realized that's what determines which priest goes on what mission before."

"Neither did I. For it is the Holy Spirit that leads and guides into all truth."

"I do not understand."

"I just learned how God orchestrates his servants here through you. I recognize this as I listen very carefully to what others speak around me. If what they speak has word of knowledge of me drawing closer to God, then it was of the Lord or not. Now as you Have spoken in the Spirit of the

Lord, 'Do you have any ideas on what I should tell them for more sparks of light to go forth?'"

"You've been so humble. Yet, you are in charge of this whole facility."

"All of my boasting is in the Lord, for He has authority here."

"Then what you say is true. I am under the guidance of the Lord."

"He is blessing you from the Northern Hills of Zion by the city of the Great King. For here is where the clouds of heaven touch the earth in glory as I have seen it before the marriage supper of the Lamb at adoration of the Holy Host where only family in place of money or position matters."

"I will share what the Lord has put within my heart. I know of the priest named Marcus. He ministered to me many years ago and is very humble. A precious soul, whereas you say that Father Jim is ambitious and has less concern for people. So, you should warn him to keep an eye on Jim who is troubled in his faith. For I have learned by what is most important from the words of the *Book of Life*, 'This is my commandment that you love one another as I have loved you, that your joy may be full.'"

"My, Honer, that is some solid counsel. Though, what if I were to tell you that much learning has filled Marcus to the point of making him prideful and impatient?"

"Then he should be tempered with love 'til the gentleness of God's honest light of truth level him off again. For I know he has a good heart."

"Would you love him for me on this trip as I know he has a good heart, too."

"Behold, I bring you glad tidings with the good news of a great joy. For, there shall be peace and goodwill to all men this day. I will do it!"

"I thank you both."

"What do you mean, both?"

"I can tell by the way you talk that you're living what you read, which can only happen by drawing from the root of the new covenant.

Know from this time forth, that a ministering angel is speaking through you and it will not only keep you well fed by the messages shared through you, but glorify Christ to others, too."

"How do you know this?"

"Rimka was my first student to teach me to remain teachable and by God's Spirit, I can tell that a similar angel speaks through you."

After spreading the word for a meeting in the forest, Eagaldorf knocks on the door to his home and hears the sound of his mother's voice bid him to come in. Once inside, he notices a look from her, but then shrugs it off in the face of meeting his aunt Louisa and uncle Eztree again. His aunt is joyous and talkative, and uncle amiable to reach out to him in an attempt to bond in love, "I see that you keep the firewood well stocked and have even managed to set a good fence around the garden, your skills could sure be used back at our village."

Luisa then buts in, "Aye! Don't pester the boy with small talk. What he needs is a hug from his aunt Luisa."

Eagaldorf looks at them both as though they were from another world, but then smiles to be polite.

His uncle makes another comment, "Seth was good enough to help me unload the wagon while you were away. You should have grain enough for the winter.”

“Oh, that is welcome news, thank you uncle Eztree.” Eagaldorf gives him a hug in response.

“Now haven’t you grown up to be a fine young man with a good stout hug, too.” He pats him on the back.

Before he can respond, Eagaldorf notices a similar look from Seth that he received from his mother earlier then looks back to her and sees the same look again, “What is going on?”

Rimka enquires after giving Seth a look who steps out the door to keep watch, “We believe that the worker you hired might be a spy and if he is, it might be better to go back to the old country rather than risk losing our lives in a war.”

“You can go, mother, but as for me, my home is here. Have we not worked the land and built a life together with father here? This place is all we have left of him. Do you really want him to become a fading memory?

What would happen if a war broke out elsewhere, would we pack up and then move again?

My dad, my work, and our sweat are here and here is where I am going to stay.

Now, how is it you consider the man I hired to be a spy?"

A knock is heard at the door. Rimka bids entrance as everyone braces themselves while determining if it be friend or foe. Trig stands in the doorway upon entering rather eager to give information on what he had just learned.

Entering the tall hills upon exiting the mountains of Zantee, Fathers Jim and Marcus are on the road along with Honer. They are traveling on horseback from the monastery of Ostrog to meet back at Rimka's in the woods.

It's been relatively quiet and Honer being closer in age to Marcus causes him to become inquisitive of something that has been on his mind, "Father Marcus, there's …"

"… I know, questions!"

"That's right, but how did you know?"

"I know nothing, except to be quiet and mind my own business and I suggest that you do the same."

"I respect what you've said and somehow love you for it."

"From that response, you remind me that I am in need to remain teachable. What answers do you seek as it seems that the Holy Spirit shows you favor?"

"Thank you for your kindness, Father Marcus. It is my desire to know just how to find the kind of peace that will bring me a stability to rest my mind once and for all."

"What causes you to believe that I can answer this question?"

"As a boy, there was not much that I could do for myself. Yet as I got older, I realized that grown-ups knew more than me. Until becoming a grown-up myself, I realized that I was limited and did not have all the answers either …"

"… So you feel that I, being a Father among other Fathers, might help you to know more than most grown-ups."

"Yes!"

"Then let us go to the Father of all Fathers in prayer and ask for wisdom."

All at once, Honer's horse stops and his eyes light with deep understanding as he speaks as an oracle with a vision of revelation, "What I have searched for I have found. There is a peace that passes beyond all understanding when it is from a spiritually stable world in the midst of our physically unstable one."

Father Marcus looks to Honer again and really focuses when he realizes what is happening.

Honer continues to speak, "We step into stability by growing through the door which Christ has opened for us, coming to Him in stages by our growth in love. He uses the bloodline of eternal life to give us stability on earth as it is in heaven that we can reach into it from our world. For having secured and preserved it with a perfect walk that we could not walk by His guiding Spirit, we are shown the way through entering baptism, which joins us again to the circle of life. Then by spilling the regeneration of His presence into time and back from eternity again, life flows through the loop of His love in return. His living blood keeps all flowing as a refreshing drink, granting any who would believe and trust the direction of His Spirit over the physical dying of flesh. All who trust to ask Him can know the privilege of knowing Him as bride to bridegroom, having an eternally resurrected reception of life inside."

Father Jim who has been riding ahead realizes that he doth not hear any hoof beats behind him and turns to find out why. He then calls to his riding companions with a wave, bidding them to come. Marcus waves back and bids him to return. Father Jim impatiently rides over with some choice words on his mind until he notices the glazed over stare on Honer. "A lay person receives revelation and not us, how is this possible?"

"Shhh! Can't you see that he has a vision of light with a stability of peace as in him there is no confusion?"

Honer speaks again, "All of creation testifies of the handiwork of a Creator."

"It is not possible for you to speak on these matters …"

Marcus responds, "… He has already!"

Honer continues, "You cannot comprehend God without first understanding the messages within creation."

Father Jim suddenly takes his arm and rouses him out of His trance, "Come on, we're fighting daylight."

Honer looks to him and says, "It is imperative that you now know that my love to you is from the point of all spiritual stability. For within a physically unstable world, we need the deepest point to hold all together in stability, which can only happen through the Holy Eucharist. For I have learned through my vision, revealed to me at the cross, that it is by Holy blood directly from our Lord that we can love in Spirit and in Truth. For in them all of creation is held together at the Holy Host."

Father Marcus becomes annoyed at Jim, "Do you represent the church or hide behind its authority for personal gain?"

"I am no Judas and I thank you for my clarity which now comes to mind. For there is a redirected focus of a love which is truly divine. Shall we stop and break bread?"

"Let us join the others first, for I am sure that everyone wants to rekindle their flames with Honer's new revelation of our consecrated Eucharistic meal."

Honer then adds, "Yes, we are fighting daylight."

Scott pulls the trigger on a crossbow and the arrow jumps across the room as all is observed by those who watch through an opened barn door. He then goes to fetch the arrow from out of a sawed off piece of tree stump and turning, he notices all who are there.

"Oh, eagledorf, I am glad of your return. As you can see, I have completed a solid example of my version of a crossbow. If you like it, I can repeat the process 'til you have ample supply. Here, give it a try."

Eagaldorf takes it in hand and after loading, takes aim and fires, hitting the stump at its center. "This is marvelous craftsmanship. Where did you ever learn how to make such a fine instrument?"

"My grandfather showed me."

"I'd like to meet him someday."

"That can be arranged."

"Perhaps he would like to band with us against our oppressor, Scott."

"A war? Perhaps after I finish with the crossbow, I can travel with your aunt and uncle when they leave here. I have no desire to stick around for a war."

"How did you know that my aunt and uncle were not from around here?"

"I did not mean to overhear, but when I was gathering wood to make arrows, I heard Seth and your uncle talking."

Seth interjects, "We were talking rather robustly at that."

"I was hoping that you would stick around as I'm sure that we could use a man of your talents."

Louisa blurts out, "At least we know that he's not a spy. For a spy would never want to leave in the heart of a war."

"A spy? You thought that I was a spy?"

Horse hooves are heard clip clopping at the barn door just behind those in the doorway.

"In all honesty, I was looking for information, but I never considered myself to be a spy."

"Out of the way," barks out Sergeant James as Trig and the others step aside.

"King Ronan, what are you doing here?"

"Fleeing the country as I fear my life may be in danger. That is if Eztree and Louisa would allow me to hitch a ride when they are ready to go."

Eagaldorf speaks in anger, "This sniveling coward is our king? You are worse than a spy. Although, I am surprised that you did not choose to have more suitable accommodations for your travels."

King Ronan exclaims, "Remarkable!"

Sergeant James goes to draw his sword, "Perhaps he needs a lesson in manners."

"No, sergeant. In fact, give me your sword in its sheath."

After disarming himself, he hands it to his king who looks to Rimka and then Back at Eagaldorf with a stare in his eyes, "Come forward and kneel before your king who has your favor in mind as you side with the truth like myself."

Eagaldorf responds by giving his king an apprehensive look, "What do you want of me?"

"If you trust in the truth of what you have spoken, make a stand or be a coward like myself," he then gestures with his hand for him to come forward and kneel once again.

Rimka holds her breath as her son walks putting one foot in front of the other and kneels before his king who draws and swings the blade, passing over his head. "I could have easily removed you from this life for your insult. Though anyone who is not afraid to speak his mind in honesty and show me loyalty the way that you just did shall share a common bond with me."

King Ronan rests the sword upon Eagaldorf's shoulder, "With this sword of court, I, King Ronan, dub thee to rise as Sir Eagleheart, high advisor to my throne. You shall now serve our people well as I see a leader in you."

The sergeant begins to speak, "Your majesty …"

"We are still at court, sergeant!"

"My pardons, majesty."

"Rimka, come forth and kneel."

Coming forth with her son now looking on, he joyfully watches his mother. "The name Rimka suits you well. So, I dub thee Rimka, Duchess of the woodlands of Eridu and a member of my council. You may rise, ma'am, who bore a son that allows your shadow of influence to rest on an Eagle's heart. Now, Sergeant James, you may share your rather pressing news."

"Your father has been mauled to death by a wild boar."

Ronan lets the sword fall into the dirt on the barn floor as his wrist turns from the sad news. It stands on end sticking up out of the ground as tears start to fill his eyes. Dropping to his knees, he lets his pain be known, "Poor father!"

Eagleheart then states while looking unto his king, "I lost my father in an accident with a boar as well." He then opens his arms and extends his hands, "I am not without feeling, your majesty." The two start to sob together while in a powerful kneeling embrace.

Everyone in the room is looking on when a vision enters Eagleheart's mind with a focused stare. He then starts to whistle a tune which quickly turns to a song, "Open my eyes, Lord … open my eyes. I need a fresh vision to meet every need. I open my hand, Lord, which opens my heart … to receive Your great Spirit with affections of love. I know and I hold You as You're in my mind … gentle Your nature which is keeping me kind. You light up my darkness and show me the way … brilliant Your glory, I have to stay. For now that I know You, there's no turning away, and by the truth of this song … I shall not run astray. I hold and adore You in deepest esteem … You fill me with life, Lord … much more than a dream. You're the Alpha, Omega … the Great I Am, too. You raise and You craft me … as I am brand new." Coming out of his trance after singing, he hears the voice of His king who releases him.

"I thank you for comforting me." On looking to his sergeant, King Ronan takes up the sword and holds it in hand, "Shhh! Take a knee."

Sergeant James is quick to comply and bows his head.

"Sergeant, as my father, King Liam, has officially passed. I am now king and dub you Sir James.

You may rise as captain of the guard and a member of my new council as well.

Eagelheart suggests, "As high counselor, I move. We have our first council meeting in the house where it's a bit warmer."

All look on and agree. Next, while exiting the barn, Sage and Benjah ride in together as the king looks on. Eaglheart picks up on his uneasiness and says, "More woodsmen arriving, my king. Now, as there is much to discuss, I want you to rest assure that they are friend and not foe."

"Are there more to arrive?"

"Sage is the largest landowner and all are in league with him and as my mother has his ear … Let's just say placing Rimka on the council was a good idea."

"And who would the other be?"

"That would be Benjah, he has a tendency to believe that he knows as much as Rimka and can be rather competitive at times due to his pride, but his heart is in the right place."

Putting up his hood, "I have an idea that might just bring all to order at our meeting."

A Turn of Events

Once inside, all gather at the table and make themselves comfortable. Benjah leads in with the first question rather abruptly, "Have you come to inquire about the poaching, sergeant?"

"Yes I have as a matter of fact. Though why not let the king open the meeting?"

"King?"

Ronan lowers his hood and says, "King Ronan at your service."

Sage questions, "But how?"

Benjah bows his head, "Pardons, Majesty."

"Let's bring this meeting to order and see if we can find out, 'what is happening in Eridu?'"

Benjah interrupts, "Majesty, would it not be advisable to send the sergeant to fetch troops from your father's court for protection from your poachers?"

Rimka's son speaks on behalf of the king, "Benjah, my name is now Eagleheart as I have been knighted to the position of chief advisor by King Ronan. It has just been learned that His father King Liam is dead and until we find out all of the circumstances as to how and why, it would not be advisable to send anybody anywhere."

Rimka comments as well, "Benjah, so you know, it will not be necessary to send Captain James of the royal guard and now royal advisor anywhere. For when he is missed at the castle, undoubtedly, others will be sent to find out what has happened to him."

"Pardons, I will listen."

Eagleheart continues, "First off, I believe Trig has a report that will be of interest to everyone present. Trig, would you be so good as to …"

"… Yes, here are my findings, 'when I was traveling the main road looking for anything out of the ordinary, I heard voices from off in the distance. I could not quite make them out, so I dismounted and quietly went on a foot so as to not disturb the brush. Then, discovering them to be camped on Sailo's property who they earlier removed, I got close enough to hear quite an earful.'"

King Ronan questions, "On behalf of us all, 'What did you learn?'"

"Plain and simple, I learned that the royal hunters are not really who they claim to be. For they boasted about how they are going to chase us off our properties and how there'd be a war that would bring a bloody time to Eridu. Someone has well paid them and offered our lands to them as a part of it as well. They laughed about all of it and how there be a traitor among your advisors at court, too."

"Then I was right to leave. Did you learn of the name of the traitor at my old court?"

"I dared not to tarry any longer. For the wind shifted and them being good hunters, they could have got my scent."

"Excellent scouting, Trig. I figure their leader has worn a hood so as to not be recognized, otherwise his name might have been mentioned."

"Eagleheart agrees, "I figure the same way, your majesty."

All eyes then turn to the captain, "Well, gents, I suspect murder in the case of King Liam due to some strong evidence."

"What did you find?" asks Ronan.

"For one, blood-covered footprints would indicate that someone watched your father die. Then when I tracked the direction from which the boar came, I found crate marks from where it was released at Liam's pass, known at one time as the valley of the dragon."

"But how did they get it to charge my father?"

"I haven't figured that out yet, but I will."

Eagleheart becomes further involved, "Majesty, it usually boils down to those who have and those who have not. If these two groups can join in a type of agreement before the Lord, like in a marriage, there can be peace again. Now consider, who would stand to gain most from a war between those at court and the woodsmen?"

Ronan responds, "That's just it, nothing seems to add up along these lines."

Sage questions, "Isn't there more than one way that someone can be poor?"

After looking to his mother, Eagleheart responds, "Yet who among us has yet to better understand the ways of the bloodline that grants resurrection?" Rimka's gaze captures her son's attention, "All right. I guess we're all still learning … even though some are faster to understand this than others." Perhaps the ones who seem distant and cold and who are lacking in love would stand out more than the others, mother."

Rimka responds, "It is true that what you are saying could have some merit, but as man looks on the outer appearance, it is God who looks upon the heart."

Eagleheart suggests, "All we would have to do is cross names among us and see if there are any agreements and these could be watched."

King Ronan speaks politely, "That sounds rather complicated and we do lack the manpower to carry out such an undertaking…"

Captain James interrupts, "… Manpower! Trig, 'How many men would you say were in their hunting camp?'"

"There were the three leaders that boasted among themselves about working for a royal advisor in laughter, for they received coin without knowledge of the king. Do the names Sirus, Coban, and Paxy mean anything to anyone?"

"That's three. Did you hear any more voices or see anyone?"

"I saw three large tents through the brush, each capable of holding a dozen men."

"That would account for the three leaders, each in charge of a dozen. Could you find your way back there in the night … if you had to, I mean?"

"I suppose I could."

Eagleheart interrupts, "Wait! There's something else we've not considered."

With all eyes upon him, Rimka questions her son, "What do you have in mind?"

"We can send Eztree for help. King Bumba is only a hard day's ride from here and if refused, King

Kelth of the Nomads is only a couple of hours from there …"

Rimka addresses the group, "You'll have to excuse my son's shortsightedness as he is not familiar with the differences of protocol of each tribe."

Ronan chuckles under his breath in response.

Eagleheart responds, "I do not understand?"

His mother continues, "Son, you can't just make such a request without showing each tribe their due respects as they have protocols that they follow. It could take you days before you would even be able to go before a council."

Eztree comments as well, "And although our tribe would be more likely to come quickly, it would still take time to gather up volunteers, without including time for preparation for a long ride for almost a week. There just isn't enough time."

"Now, I understand."

King Ronan interrupts, "Wait before this goes any further, there is something else that you should know."

Captain James questions, "And what would that be?"

"Pine, the magistrate knows that I'm here. If we were to wait for Gray to return who is due back at any time, a meeting could be organized in Eridu that would expose what is happening."

The captain is quick to respond, "Your majesty, is Gray overdue on his return?"

"Now that you mention it, he is a little bit late in getting back."

Captain James is bold in what he proclaims, "Can't you see that he is probably being held against his will and being prevented from his return?"

Eagleheart surmises the situation, "It is obvious that there is a masterplan that is unfolding before us.

Calington Castle is cut off from us, a war is trying to be sparked between the royal palace and us woodsmen, and Gray has disappeared, perhaps it is time for King Ronan to return to the palace."

Captain James draws his sword and spikes the end of the table, "And I say nay! Can't you see that King Ronan has been missed by now and if he is being watched for, he'll be murdered upon return and then the blame would fall on the woodsmen anyway?

Your strange disappearance can even suggest on the morrow that you've been kidnapped as well with similar results. I say the time to act is now as we still have the element of surprise."

Eagleheart then comments, "What if it's a trap to lure us in for a massacre? Perhaps Trig overheard intentionally ..."

"We can divide into two groups. Then if the first group is overrun, the second would still have an element of surprise as reinforcements."

King Ronan grants the captain's request, "Splendid! Seeing how night is almost upon us, what would you suggest, James?"

The captain starts a count, "How many men have you, Sage?"

... All at once, a darkness falls upon Eagleheart, and then the spirit of Lexure the demon comes out from his eye and begins to whisper in his ear. *"A king befriends a common woodsman, he has picked you for his amusement. You're no more than a court jester to him, for he did not choose your ideas! He chose Captain James' campaign over your advice when you're supposedly the chief advisor."* Taken by surprise, this dark voice goes unnoticed as Eagleheart has been clueless about being caught off guard before God when making his prideful promise to vow never to eat boar again.

Rimka picks up on her son being downcast and asks, "Eagleheart, have you made any promises without considering our Lord as of late?"

He fights through a sudden dimness of the dark within his mind and responds to his mother, "None that I know of."

The captain interrupts after overhearing, "Woman, if you have a private matter to discuss with your son, might it wait 'til after we finish our council for war?"

"Can't you tell that our chief advisor is not attentive to what you are saying?"

"Let me repeat it then. Well, lad, Sage says he has fifteen men working for him that are fit for war, but not all can be trusted. So, I say we use them at first attack without telling them about our plans for reinforcements."

Rimka becomes involved, "Honer has still not checked in."

"Now, who would Honer be?"

"He has gone for the clergy at the monastery in Ostrog, for if the church were with us, maybe we could have an alternative plan."

"Putting their lives in danger is not my idea of a plan," says Captain James.

"Perhaps my son has some further counsel on this matter."

Eagleheart feels the sting of his mother's words of love as painful when entering into his thoughts. He then responds with a slight change in his voice as it is Lexure which speaks through him in the discomfort of his darkness that now resides, *"Must you always press me, for I prefer being alone right now."*

A cluster of hoof beats are heard arriving outside the cabin door followed with a knock on it.

Rimka says, "One moment please," as the king puts up his hood while the others take defensible positions around the room, all but her son who seems impervious as to what is happening. The

Captain then goes to the door and steadies himself to draw his sword before opening it. Honer is the first to step into the dimly lit room while Rimka lights some large candles on the table, bringing more light to the situation. This reveals two priests standing behind him with their beaded crosses hanging down from their robes. Marcus recognizes Rimka's son and calls out to him, "Eagaldorf, why are you so downcast?"

Lexure speaks through him again, *"My name is eagleheart!"*

King Ronan blurts out from under his hood, "Perhaps he has gone into deep grief over the loss of his father as my father was killed by a boar this day to remind him, too."

Lexure speaks in a low tone of voice through the chief counselor's thoughts, *"Shhh! The boar is now a secret!"* Eagleheart rises straight up from his despondent position in his seat to standing upright before all, *"I feel a need to go for the crossbow and practice a bit in the barn."*

Marcus sternly says, "Oh, no you don't, demon! I adjure you to tell me your name in the presence of the Lord Jesus Christ of Nazareth, right now?"

The captain stands in front of the doorway between him and Marcus, saying, "Listen to the priest!" All at once, Captain James finds himself grabbing at his throat while being choked as he is raised against the open door. Father Jim starts praying his rosary beads as Marcus starts to give authoritative commands, "Everyone in this room is to be silent and not say a word."

Father Jim prays in the background, "Hail Mary, full of grace. The Lord is with you. Blessed are you among women and blessed is the fruit of thy womb, Jesus …"

Marcus holds up his cross, "Under the authority of The Lord Jesus Christ, you are rebuked!" Captain James falls to the floor gasping for air.

Father Jim continues, "… Holy Mary mother of God, pray for us sinners now and at the hour of our death. Amen."

"What is your name and what is your purpose here?"

"I was sent by Your master and Lord with special permission to do him in and receive his soul as my reward."

Father Marcus calmly approaches and extends his cross over the boys face, "By the blood of The Christ, 'What is your name?'"

After a loud bellowing cough, it gives its identity, "My name is Lexure!"

Jim's voice is heard in the background, "Hail Mary, full of grace. The Lord is with you …"

Marcus hold's the cross with Jesus upon it, deeming Him as a more intimate friend even closer than before, "Lexure, by the blood of Christ, you are now silenced!"

"Blessed are you among women and …"

"Eagleheart, how did you make a pact with the devil?"

Crying in a whimpering tone of voice, he responds, "I don't know!"

"… Blessed is the fruit of thy womb, Jesus …"

Marcus has a revelation, "It was said by Lexure that the Boar was a secret. You must ponder this 'til it is revealed what this means."

"I can't do it!"

"… Holy Mary, mother of God. Pray for us sinners now …"

"Yes, you can! Lexure is lying to you."

"… and at the hour of our death, Amen!"

"Did you vow any vows that excluded God's help?"

"Hail Mary, full of grace. The Lord is with you …

"Wait a minute! In my pride, I vowed never to eat boar again."

"I want you to repeat after me …"

"The boy nods his head *yes*.

"… Blessed are you among women and …"

Marcus continues, "… I renounce the vow I vowed in my pride never to eat boar meat again."

"… blessed is the fruit of thy womb, Jesus."

Eagleheart repeats, "I renounce the vow I vowed in my pride never to eat boar meat again by the blood of Jesus."

"… Now and at the hour of our death. Amen!

"Quickly, take my hand and pray with me. Our Father who art in heaven hallowed be thy name.

Thine kingdom come, Thine will be done on earth as it is in heaven, give us this day our daily bread and forgive us our trespasses as we forgive those who trespass against us. Keep us from every temptation and deliver us from evil. Amen" Father Marcus pulls the boy to his breast and embraces him with a loving hug 'til a Holy restful smile appears on his face.

"Eagleheart is now lost to you, Lexure. We are now found sharpened by this boy's countenance of our Lord's more brilliant light than your darkness. You are now cast out to go back to the abyss from which you came as you've been renounced by the authority of the truth of Jesus name."

The candles suddenly flicker towards the direction of the door which closes shut by itself and then a peaceful presence fills the room. Eagleheart's face suddenly shines forth, brighter than the candles that light the atmosphere and a joyous laugh spreads to everyone as all light with delight.

Rimka is smiling just as brightly as her son and while aglow, speaks a word of knowledge from the Lord, "King Ronan, wisdom now tells me that you were no coward before. Your leaving the woods to keep Eridu from falling must happen. You shall leave this province at once."

The Ransom Note

$\mathcal{A}$t the absence of King Ronan, "The Ten" hold a secret meeting in the same room as before.

Gunta announces, "Our king seems to have evaded us, so I've called you here to find a resolution to this matter."

Swan becomes bold, "We could send word to our men and have him struck down at once."

Paps questions, "Then how would it become known that the woodsmen are to blame?

Swan suggests, "We could place his body on their roads and let a legitimate royal party which is hunting discover him."

Link calls out, "I say we collect ransom and keep it for ourselves!"

Scorch gets involved, "Animals would probably devour him first."

Thortan becomes jovial, "He ought to know as he's king of the beasts."

Scorch becomes angry and clenches his fists, "I've killed men for less than that!"

Gordy counters with a calming effect, "If it comes down to battle, he's liable to save your life, he's a brother to us Scorch."

Releasing his breath slowly and unclenching his fists, he calmly walks over to Thortan and extends his large hand. Thortan takes it with a smile and Scorch pats him on the back so hard he practically knocks the wind out of him purposefully, "I feel ya brother."

Wilaxe laughs spitting out some ale all over everyone, "That's the way I like it, real camaraderie."

Dunge blatantly blurts out, "I want to kill, I need to see blood!"

Gunta shakes his head at the whole scene and Sekco, picking up on this says, "You've had your fun, gents, now lets get back to the order of the business at hand. How are we going to explain King Ronan's strange disappearance?"

Swan then States, "Wait! I see how we can use his disappearance to our advantage."

Gunta asks in an inquisitive manner, "How?"

Swan responds, "If we make a ransom note and claim it to be from the land owners of the woods, then we could be done with King Ronan."

Gunta gets everyone's attention, "Men. Send word that if King Ronan turns up, his life is to end. Quietly, when by himself, no witnesses of course."

A full moon lights the road. Louisa rides in a lone wagon with a young passenger by her side who has his hood up. All at once, they hear hoof beats approaching them from behind which disturbs their travels. Then they are upon them and as one rider pulls up alongside, the other grabs the reins stopping the horses. The uniforms of the royal hunters are noticed in the moonlight.

The man by the wagon says, "State your business."

Louisa responds, "Me and my nephew are heading back home after visiting my sister. 'What's this all about?"

"What would the name of your sister be?"

"Rimka."

"Okay, you are free to go. Oh, one more thing, would your majesty mind lowering your hood?"

Out of reflex, he reaches for his hood.

"It is him!" says the other hunter.

The man at the wagon says, "We've been sent to escort you safely back to the palace, your majesty."

"I wasn't up for travel anyway." Lowering his hood and turning his head to the side before forward again sends a signal.

Arrows sing out striking the imposters that fall from their horses.

"How did you know that these men where not legitimately here for you?" asks Louisa.

"A matter of protocol."

"I do not understand."

"They did not present papers from the magistrates office. They would have offered to take me to Pine as we have an agreement to sift through any attempt on my life. Be thankful of what they were trying to do as they showed you a courtesy."

"I still do not understand."

"They sought to spare your life to not be killed as a witness to my death."

Riders come up the main trail that were hanging way back from the wagon. "Well, at least we know for certain that it's safer for you to flee than remain and fight as assassins have undoubtedly been hired to kill you."

Marcus, who is among the riders, speaks up, "I'm coming with you."

"You should be with the men, they need you more."

"We shall hold prayer now, then the raid on the enemy camp shall be a blessed success and if any are wounded or killed, they could be brought to Father Jim who is with Rimka."

"Very well then, your company will be most welcome. It should make for some interesting conversation. Now, how are we to pray?"

Marcus replies, "Where two or more are gathered in my name, there am I in your midst. We are to pair up in groups of twos and threes. Then after sharing all that is praise worthy to edify each other, we are to bear one another's burdens in prayer, quietly and in order, praying for each other. Every person to the right of you shall bear the burden of the other on hearing requests and express it to the Lord. The one who prays first shall report anything that sticks out in the mind as exceptional and tell eagleheart who will report it to me and then I will share it to edify all."

King Ronan suggests, "You shall count off 1-2-3 in sequence, then all like numbers shall come together. Since sage is already en-route to the enemy camp with his men, Marcus will pray for them in my group to save us time."

Marcus makes a final statement, "Seeking ambition through prayer is treason with the Lord, so as not to put yourselves in danger, quiet yourself and wait on the Lord for His humble Spirit to pray through you, He will come."

The king signals that it is time and the counting begins among the reinforcements. There is a buzz of prayer that is heard throughout the men while

Louisa, Ronan, and Marcus share their burdens and pray, too.

Marcus shares his concern for the men, then Ronan as well and then Louisa is heard, "Oh, Lord, I thank you for showing us favor with the assassins. I am now concerned for our travels to our village. I am troubled, help us."

Marcus waits upon the Lord and responds accordingly, "Lord I ask that you ease our minds. He then speaks a verse from the *Book of Life*, "If the Lord is with us then what manner of beast or peril shall prevail as we can do all things through Christ who strengthens us."

Eagleheart soon reports to Marcus after hearing from the group leaders saying, "The men have all drawn closer and are encouraged by the Lord, this eve."

Marcus then proclaims to all the men, "We shall prevail, for the Lord is with us."

"Captain James announces to king Ronan, "It is best that you three get going, I'll have a white flag sent to your tribe, Louisa, when it is safe for King Ronan to return."

The Captain turns his attention to his men. Now that the King is under a blanket that covers the supplies for the trip, Marcus sits in his place next to Louisa, and the wagon pulls away.

Arriving at the enemy camp, the reinforcements shoot arrows hitting the fake royal hunters, which stand out in their colorful uniforms by their bonfire. Once subdued, names are taken and it is discovered that two of the leaders and ten men have survived the war after being captured.

The leaders, Sirus and Coban, are interrogated with ankles bound and hands tied behind their backs while sitting pressed against each other back to back. Captain James begins to inquire of them, "I want to know who hired you and where Grey is being held."

There is no answer.

The captain continues, "Coban and Sirus, I have my sources to know that you two are the remaining leaders."

Sirus smirks and says, "Then why not use your sources to inform you of what you need to know?"

Captain James calmly answers, "You have ten remaining men who are unharmed at the moment. That leaves me with ten different ways of how I am going to deal with you. Now as one of you is expendable, you'll have to decide between the two of you which will be tortured first." The Captain then says, "Bring the first man and steady him."

James then goes to the bonfire and removes a red hot poker made of iron. He proceeds to walk to the man and starts to lift it to his eyes 'til he cries out, "No, please don't blind me!"

Coban quickly proclaims, "I'll talk as there's no sense in blinding this man now that I see what will happen to us, for our cause is not just."

"Alright, where is Gray being held?"

Coban answers the captain, "There is a small village just after the mountains of Zantee on the road to Ostrog, he is being held in a large barn in one of the stalls to keep him concealed."

"How many men, Sirus?"

"Why ask me when it seems you have a source of information?"

"Only dead men tell no tales."

"There are three!"

"Now Sirus, who hired you?"

"I don't know his name or even what he looks like."

"You disappoint me."

"Coban gets involved, "No, it's true as he wore a hooded mask according to Paxy and his lieutenant."

"How were you summoned to meet Him?"

Coban motions with his hand towards Paxy, the third leader who is laying on the ground, "As you say, dead men tell no tales."

The captain answers, "Those who live in darkness have no light of life to see as well."

Sirus further asks, "What do you mean by that?"

"I am learning that the warmth of love sparks light when it is from the Creator of all."

"Perhaps when time permits, I can better understand what you're talking about," says Sirus.

Captain James smiles, "Now is the appointed time, for you have been paid a wage to be a slave against your conscience. Yet, wisdom is more precious than rubies or diamonds and more costly than gold. For what good is money without knowing how to spend it on what brings true life."

An inquisitive Sirus questions further, "I do not understand?"

"Life cannot be found enjoyable when discontent as was my case 'til I found love and truth to balance out in the form of a man. The Creator had a Son who's name is Jesus Christ and clarity of mind has come for me by meeting Him in His love."

Coban interjects, "You tell us of love and yet you threatened us with violence. This is not understood."

"The key word is threaten as it was just a suggestion on my part."

"So, if you claim to love, then why not set us free?"

"I am working on doing that right now, for when your minds are free, you shall prefer light and life over the darkness and death which you are inviting to live within you."

"How can this be?" asks Sirus.

"When the light of truth of God's love comes in, you will be set free from the pains that are causing you to hate life. For within the dimness of thoughts after trying everything which causes you to see lies, this is where all seems unkind by creatures living inside a frozen and unfeeling mind."

"Being without feelings must be true, for how else could I not see my cruelty to others unless a part of me was missing.

"It is only by the warmth of God's love that light comes to thaw feelings and make you alive."

"How do I receive such love that comes from The Creator to free my mind?"

"First you must understand that this is where the real battle lay, or you will continue to defy rather than be reconciled to God. It is He, who by the righteous act of His own power, justifies a bloodline which endorses all to be alive with a life that thrives. Him being gracious with us is what sets all men free. So, wait and see that gratitude shall cause you to bow a knee."

"How can this be?" asks Coban.

"He offers us pure blood by the sacrifice of His Son and when partaken it in a worthy humble manner by desiring new life through trusting in Him, our darkness leaves where we were missing in sin. No longer will you miss His light which prevents a mind from going dim. For His merciful Kingdom opens and lets us in when we stop seeking a name for ourselves and worship Him."

Corban and Sirus enquire together, "Where can this pure blood be found that we two might have a bond with Him?"

"God, the Creator of heaven and earth provides it for us, restoring all to order by a power called resurrection and this is what raises the dead. It grants every man eternal life who chooses to follow a path that unties all knots of darkness where minds went dim. Choose to follow and the brilliant truth that lights all understanding will come by Him."

Sirus becomes doubtful, "A light of truth that unties dark knots, raising from the dead to eternal life, do you expect me to believe in a child's story?"

Rimka's son becomes involved, "My name once was Eagaldorf and when I believed as a child, a seed of truth and love came into being with level sight to see His light from beyond the above. I have now grown mature by His same Spirit of light, enough for Him to change my name to Eagleheart."

"Enough of this nonsense!" says Sirus.

Eagleheart continues, "Was it nonsense when you poached my dear the other day? For when I was known as Eagaldorf, I could have killed you for what you did and now that I have the advantage I do not.

"I thought I recognized you. Go ahead and have your advantage, for I can see now that I am as good as dead anyway."

"If I were Eagaldorf, yes, but now as my character has changed to Eagleheart, I can say that I love you through the forgiveness of your own shortsightedness, for you have thoughts in the dimness of your mind that have been telling you what to do. Now you have a choice to continue to obey them by the coins that you serve in your darkness or trade them in for the light of wisdom that will dispel 'em. For when God's warming love thaws your heart for you to feel, you'll see by God's light what is truly real."

Captain James speaks again, "We have a *Book of Life* that states, 'Unless you become as a little child, you shall not inherit the kingdom of God.'"

Sirus looks to his men and sees that they have been listening, too. "Let me talk to my men as they have heard what's been said concerning this matter. If questions arise, we can then ask them accordingly?"

"Feel free to talk openly among yourselves, for when truth is spoken, it fans the fire of God's love."

Sirus calls to the others, "Men, if you have been listening to what's been said, are there any questions that you may have to help us all better understand?"

One of them calls out, "How do I find The Creator that I may know Him in worship, too?"

"All men are justified by faith through believing that God's word testifies of the sacrifice of His own pure blood which lives forever. For we die in sin while missing Him by being filled where we were lacking as His bloodline holds complete life and ours doth not."

"Coban asks, "How do you receive this faith that you speak of?"

The captain explains, "By partaking of the sacrifice of justice and believing that the Body, Blood, Soul, and Divinity of the Lord Jesus Christ, Son of the Creator is alive. He will abide with you on earth as He is in heaven. Faith dictates that the testimony found in the *Book of Life* testifies of a New Covenant, which practices a sacrifice through what is called a Holy meal of the Host of presence. We meet God in a state of thanksgiving at His altar through this perpetual belief when connected to His vine. His life is transferred to us and transforms us all by the action of His power as He is the gate between heaven and earth. He keeps us connected to Him as the door by which we draw a bloodline that is alive from the fruit of His living vine."

Another man suddenly calls out, "I know what I have and will continue on in what is familiar to me as you have no proof of what you're saying to be true."

Eagleheart interjects, "Doth it not take you faith to worship the god's of arrogance and pride which has blinded your mind from a light that satisfies? I speak to you in a humble place as I have died to these lesser spirits to come alive. For I delight in worshiping the God of light by the warmth of His truth that tells of His love which lives within the essence of His being. Proof is in the hearing that my word's ring true and that my character has changed. For once where I sought to be vengeful, now I am tame."

James points to the rising sun, "Draw close to the sacrifice of God's love and escape the shallows of shadow in layers of greed by coin and go to where understanding comes. I say to you when you comprehend the deep, eternity brings life, one you will know by the contentment of it being new forever."

"I do find myself dissatisfied with what life has to offer and wanting more is no solution for sure."

Putting down his arm, James says, "Then why not pray to join us and surrender your pride that you can try the Spirit of God and see that He is good?"

"… And then what?"

"Once you see that He is good, He will instruct you on what to do next by messenger angels that will speak to your thoughts and enlighten your mind to receive life by His love."

"I want to receive this love and know its warmth that leads out of darkness by the light of His life, too."

"When darkness goes as God's light comes in, love will replace your hate and you will feel this within. Though the battle will be fierce when pressing in, you'll eventually sense when God goes missing, you need to learn in times of darkness to look away from your ways and call on Him. So, persevere to know all of God's truth throughout this real war of sin until He no longer goes missing within."

Eagleheart then asks, "What is your name, corporal?"

"I go by Duff."

"Well, Duff, are you ready for a change that shall open your eyes to the sight of eternal light and take you out from the coolness of what is dark?"

"How will this happen? I mean, will it be painful?"

"Only to the land owner that is keeping you imprisoned inside your soul, but for you, it shall be a glorious joy when receiving the breath of life which will come in by the light of love."

"What must I do to be redeemed out of my darkness to own my own soul in the property of this kingdom of light?"

"Duff, have you ever noticed the differences between calm winds of peace and the chaos of the dark clouds during a raging storm?"

"Yes. I know what you're talking about as my thoughts race within my mind, leaving me unsettled at times."

"The winds tell of spirits that unkindly drive you on as in the waves of motion there is no rest for a soul. For like the fire of a flame being released from its source, only ash of dust remains when carried away by the wind in the end."

"Then how do I come out of the wind that I may find peace from the light of warmth by God's love within?"

"I want all who want to know the answer to Duff's question to raise their hands." All hands sprout up in the air to the light of a morning sun.

"So you'll understand, I want you to have stability in the framework of creation. You may put your hands down now, yet do not let them retract back into the dark but continue to hold onto the truth of my words, for they are light." The hands go down with clenched fist held to their hearts.

"Know that your days are like the size of your hand in the motion of a single breadth and are only a part of the larger one that passes through time. For time is a great wave in the commotion inside all lengths of days. All these events of motion must be broken by quieting yourselves within. Then kept in the light of eternal life where you'll not be blown out from existence while inside God's presence, His seed gets planted in us. We erupt like volcanoes with eternal life and disrupt the wave in all of time which calms the oceans of commotion in life."

Captain James gets involved again, "In the Spirit of stillness, a *Book of Life* was written to put an end to all of the commotion found in the wave of time. 'Be still and know that I am God' is one of its verses. For while in the motion of time, all is self destruction with an abuse that causes us to want to seek comfort."

Eagleheart is quick to continue, "Do not get distracted. I want everyone to know that prayer is slowing down to create a friction that sparks a heat to light a fire unto God's light of life which breaks through all that is dark. For when the framework of all creation is known, it makes it easier to join the Creator as His adorned bride while receiving Him in the intimacy of His quiet stillness. Now I want everyone to focus their minds on quieting themselves to come out of the motion of time."

After a season of settling in, Duff calls out, "Just how still do I need to be?"

"Stiller then a soft breeze on the silence of a rose petal and then stiller still. For God's voice of love is so gentle that unless you are absolutely still, His seed cannot break through the motion of the soil of a hardened heart."

"Who then can know God?"

"With Him all things are possible. I will pray for His love to touch all of you. Then any who feel led to do so may pray with me afterwards. Oh Lord, these men thirst and are hungry for Your love. Please hear the cry of their hearts and honor them with Your answer.

Now with a still and quiet soul before the Lord, I want you to focus on the light of the truth of my words. My Creator, by the Son of your pure blood, give me Your new and eternal life on earth as it is in heaven in the name of Jesus Christ, that my darkness be cast out by His sacrifice."

James takes over after a few moments, "Breathe in deep and know His love as all be bright by the warmth of His affection. Now through the door of Him who is true, return them to the love of all and be made new."

All then take the breath that leads to life and experience the Lord's great price for peace.

On the Road

The sun hangs just before noon in the sky as the wagon bounces and bumps along while its being drawn. Louisa is at the reins while driving the horses at a quarter pace with Marcus by her side. All at once, loud snoring is heard from the back of the wagon underneath the large blanket that covers King Ronan who's among the supplies.

Riders are heard on the approach, but it is undetermined if they are going to ride alongside them or pass on by. A quick decision by Marcus, causes him to grab the horse prodder from Louisa and shout, "Stop abusing your horses, all they really need is a few kind words." He then tosses the horse whip in the back which disrupts Ronan from his sleep and he quickly stops his loud nap.

Soon after, three angry looking riders approach the wagon and begin to inquire of them, "About how long have you been on the road?"

Marcus speaks up, "Why do you ask?"

"My name is Cleave. This is Blackie and the man beside him is Spike." All nod their heads and smile deceitfully as though they were bidding them a good day. Cleave continues to speak, "Were looking for a friend of ours, he'd be a young strapping lad about five and a half feet tall. Have you seen anyone like that on the road during your ride … ah, where did you say you were from?"

Marcus replies, "We're just passing by Ostrog as I'm from the Monastery."

Cleave further inquires, "How bout you, ma'am?"

Marcus interrupts, "Why not join us on our journey and we can discuss it while we reach the monastery. You can rest from your travels there for a night if need be."

"Thanks, but we'll be stopping at the small village just on the other side of this mountain pass."

"These are the mountains of Zantee and I'm sure you'll find that the village is just as suitable a place to stop as well."

"What do you have in the wagon?"

"We carry only what is necessary for our ride."

"Fair enough," says Cleave. "Come on, gents, we have an appointment to keep." They ride on ahead.

Back at Rimka's, warm smiles are aglow as lives have been changed. Father Jim is instructing all who have gathered around him in the barn. All at once, a cloud fogs his mind. He loses his train of thought by some distractions that have entered him, *"Aren't you sitting pretty with all these new students. Now you will be recognized and advance in the church at last. Invite them to come back to the monastery with you and you'll have a showing among the others that could elevate you into being the next Monsignor."*

Father Jim looks at his new students through his thoughts and says, "Pay attention, we have an adversary that infiltrates our minds and tries to gain access into them by entering all with a great divide. I am certain that this is how you were hired as recruits into a war by the coin, which has left you without any real integrity or conviction with cause.

Darkness is always trying to put out light through division from a high spiritual vantage point, but it is not above our Lord's as He is the highest authority over and beyond this world. He is The Father of lights which shapes minds as He comes down from above. For in the formation of ideas, seductions come, preventing rulers from receiving the crown of His life by warmth from His love. All thoughts of conquest get introduced, though once the true spiritual enemy is realized, lies of darkness are resolved in every conflict that causes the truth to bleed in flesh by God's own love for us until all be exposed.

Those who walk in the dark are unaware that they are being shaped into evil due to a pride that says, 'I have to survive,' as there is no trust in the protocol of God's kingdom when all is dark. Listen my beloved brothers, for in truth that's who you are as the scriptures say, 'This is my commandment that you love one another as I have loved you that your joy may be full,' so pray for all leaders that you do not know so they will come into the knowledge of God's love, too."

Taking all this in, Coban responds, "When I prayed back at our camp along with everyone else, we were all touched, but now I see the door begins to close. What must we do for it to remain open? For now I see all are in need to enter a full relationship with our new God who is the king of light that shines from within. I now know His Kingdom, too, and it is the solution."

"Yes! That's right."

Sage bursts out with the realization, "You mean we did not have to spill blood during this conflict?"

Honer becomes involved as well, "Soldiers in the Lord's army fight through prayer until they are given direction by God as to what source of action they are to take. You and your men killed to save lives, so there be no guilt upon your heads."

Sage responds, "But we did not seek God's favor for Him to give us a strategy. We struck without warning. So with a parlay, they might have surrendered sooner than later."

Honer answers, "You have learned a valuable lesson here."

"I seem to lack understanding."

"When fear replaces faith it is easy to lose sight of God in the heat of a battle and choose your own way. So you must entreat God to become more a part of your life that you will no longer rely on yourself."

Sage slowly nods his head, "Yes, I shall do this. I am grateful for the wisdom you've taught me this day."

Father Jim interjects, "I want you all to remember this well, the men who died chose to serve the coin rather than God. There is the strong possibility that you served as his agents of vengeance before He showed mercy as the men who sit here are the results of this battle, too."

The Captain raises his hand among the others and is recognized, "Father Jim, I feel the time is right for you to go to the castle at Calington."

"How so?"

"It has just been learned that King Liam has been slain and while you're comforting the family, it would be good to discern the situation at the castle."

"What situation?"

"It is not known if Prince Edward has ambitions for the crown and things for King Ronan will not be safe until we've ruled out every possibility of corruption."

"What about these men here? Who will instruct them?"

"At sun up, some of us will be leaving for a small village on the other side of the mountains of Zantee. It's not far to the Monastery from there and afterward …"

Honer interrupts, "… I wouldn't mind going back there for the sake of the men, for it is necessary for them to learn the protocol of the new kingdom they are in. Perhaps if I were to ride along with you and guide them, it would save you some time; that is if the men are in agreement."

The men look at one another and nod with smiles.

Father Jim agrees as well, "All is understood by God … and as I can see how He has the better plan, I will go to the castle on the morrow."

Sirus comments, "Father Jim, your words have stirred a new attitude within me. It is now my desire to help overcome the guards where Grey is being held. If I order those who guard him to stand down and be relieved of their duty by replacements, then after they go, the prisoner can easily be released. All can be resolved without any loss of life in a peaceful manner. Afterward, I can turn Gray loose and the men with me can join the others at the monastery.

Eagleheart and Captain James look to one another in a questioning way that suggests to each other, can he really be trusted? Honer picks up on this and says, "Jesus came to serve and not be served, being full of life and truth as a light to us all that we may have purpose in His kingdom. This is what keeps us alive on earth as it is in heaven and Sirus seems to have picked up on this."

Sirus responds, "I didn't know how to express what you just said, but what truly brings eternal life to my heart is my intention."

Eagleheart questions, "How will we find out from Paxy's lieutenant who hired you?"

"I will tell him that Captain Paxy lost his life in battle and needs to contact our leader to give report. Then I will tell him that the men are regrouping and he is needed to replace his commander when he finds them. He shall tell me the meeting place and then we can determine what to do next."

Afterward, Captain James nods to Eagleheart and says, "Then it's settled, we shall take this plan of action on the morrow."

Passing the monastery, Marcus and Ronan are discussing whether to stop. "If we stop, my king, there is the possibility of an assassin catching up to us before you are well concealed at Louisa's village. Have faith God will see us through."

Ronan speaks from beneath the blanket, "Well, I suppose if you were to rest while Louisa drove and you switched off, we could continue to move."

Louisa enquires of their faith, "How is it that faith seems to come so easily for you two? All I see are my struggles and cannot seem to get victory no matter how hard I try."

Marcus answers, "It is not for us to try, but rely on surrendering to His Spirit 'til a trust comes which will carry you like floating on the water within a rest that recognizes gratitude while in service to Him.

"So, it's not about me anymore as to look at myself while in His service, but to look at Him with a focus that no longer lets me see me."

Marcus replies, "Yes and this is where you'll learn to find rest in being carried by His peace."

The assassins have finished leaving words of discord among the people concerning King Liam's death. The villagers now believe that all of the provinces will crumble without the king being alive to keep order. They start to leave the village and pass by Captain James who appears to be there on some business. One goes for his knife, but when he sees Sage and some other men are with him, the three decide to leave the village and go elsewhere to sow more words of discord.

After James discerns the tone of disarray in the village, some of them approach him for advice. Trevor, the village leader next stands before him with others right behind and questions, "We were told by some men that recently passed through here that King Liam is dead and there is no longer order throughout the provinces. What have you to say about this, my fine soldier of the king?"

James is quick to respond, "Have you a priest in this village?"

Another villager calls out, "That would be Thomas."

"Let us go to him and have council."

Trevor volunteers, "I will take you to him right away."

The village leader presses through the crowd and by the time he reaches the church, most of the villagers of Ostrog are right behind him.

Trevor turns to the crowd after motioning to Captain James for him to follow, "Wait here. We wouldn't want to overcrowd the church." Sage and his men remain with the others.

They walk up some steps and upon reaching the door, Thomas, having overheard the crowd, greets them at the door. "What is going on, Captain?"

Captain James speaks softly, "It is best we talk inside."

The remnants of a card game is going on when Sirus walks into the barn. Paxy's lieutenant is sitting on a stool collecting some coin off of a large anvil. He then looks up from his seat and makes eye contact with his superior with two men behind him dressed in their uniforms. The lieutenant enquires, "Why have you come?"

"There was a battle between us and the woodsmen. Captain Paxy was killed and the men have scattered. You are needed to lead your men as most of your group escaped alive. Find them and I'm sure that they'll regroup."

"So, you're here to relieve me?"

"Yes."

The lieutenant rises and says, "Come on men, it's time to go to war."

"I need to know two things before you go."

"What would that be?"

"In case something should happen to you, who are we working for in order to get paid?"

"We are working for a secret society called, 'The Ten.' Every half and full moon, a man with a hooded mask rides by to receive report by the opening of the path to the woods. If no one shows, he returns keeping watch until we make contact. When a war officially breaks out between the palace guards in Eridu and the woodsmen, we are to be paid. Now, what is your second question?"

"Where are you holding Gray?"

"Come with me."

Sirus follows behind the lieutenant who directs him towards a horse stall, "Take a look under the blanket in the back."

Gray is seen tied and gagged underneath the blanket in the rear of the stall. He then drops the blanket and says, "We're all set here."

After the other men leave, Sirus turns to Duff and says, "Check the door." He then walks over to the stall and looks back to get the signal that all is clear. A single nod lets him know that all is well.

He next goes to the back of the stall and uncovers Gray. Making eye contact with him, Gray is assured by what he's been longing to hear, "We've come to get you out of here." He then takes out a knife and cuts his ropes as the third man brings him over some water to drink.

Father Thomas walks out the front door to the church and announces to the crowd from the steps, "I want you all to know that King Liam did not die in vain. For by the truth of the way that he lived his life testifies to the truth of God who is first and foremost your way of life as well. I want you to remember him in this light as he has continually pointed you all to 'The Christ' and not Himself. I know that his love for the truth helped to fashion all of our lives, …"

Someone from the people cries out, "… But he was our deliverer!"

"… Yes! Though what did he deliver you up to? I tell you that ultimately it was the truth which he carried in his heart by the Spirit of the living God that has fashioned you into being God's child. For He not only holds you, but will keep all our provinces together throughout Calington. So, if we continue to stand by the warmth of God's love which sparks forth light by His truth, no dark lie will be able to wrestle us away from Him who embraces so deeply within. No, not peril, nor diversion, not even death shall separate us from the love God that holds us. Remember, we are His children, crafted by His own light from even before we were born. He knows us all as The Father of light itself and nothing shall cause me to forget Him as should be the case with you as well. Now let us return His affection with a shout offering from all of us that He will know that He has not been forgotten." Thomas raises his fist and shouts, "I love You!" over and over 'til the crowd shouts with the Lord's confidence as one voice.

With all resolved outside, Captain James feels moved to pray within the church, "Lord, send an angel to speak to king Ronan of what has happened here." His thought is then carried by a messenger of light which appears to king Ronan from underneath the blanket on the wagon as a vision.

Some of the warriors from Bumbaland suddenly appear on the road from out of the brush. This causes the horses to rear when surprised and Louisa stops the wagon to settle them down.

Marcus calls out to them and inquires, "What brings you two out to the main road?"

"I, Naphtali, speaks for Sambu who has received a vision of King Liam dying not too long ago. He was instructed to come out to the main road and await further instruction just moments ago. Sorry for startling your horses. Your arrival tells me his vision is true. Do you have a word?"

King Ronan jumps out from under the blanket covering the supplies after overhearing, "I just had a vision from a messenger angel, wanting all provinces to know that although my father Liam has died, he still holds to the one that carries all life.

God will keep order by remembering that the relationship that my father had with the love of our Lord's truth still holds true. It even bears a light, which cuts through all darkness to feed us His life. This was the mission of King Liam as our deliverer, which still speaks to us from beyond the grave and a new message that I must carry to all of the other provinces as well. This is the stability that will preserve peace for us all and a message which I King Ronan shall deliver. With the news of my father dying delivered to Bumbaland, I am brought to see the reality of things more deeply. I am determined to share how he lived his life for covenant truth and shall continue to speak of his testimony that concerns the firm and level foundation of love for all."

Eye to Eye

$\mathcal{T}$he sun is three o'clock high in the sky and Father Jim takes in the atmosphere of Calington Castle in a discerning way. After careful observation of his actions, Prince Edward catches his eye and they wind up staring at each other. When all is said and done. The prince next comments to the Father, "Friend or foe?"

Jim responds, "What do you mean?"

"Are you trying to discern me and my family by the flesh or the Spirit of the living God and to what purpose?"

Feeling the weight of how he is to answer, before a member of the royal family, he lacks in discernment. So, he becomes a little uneasy and rests on his authority in the church when answering,

"God's kingdom is always looking to increase the flock of His church …"

"… But to what purpose? For thus says the Lord, 'I'd rather you be hot or cold as the lukewarm I will spew out of My mouth.' You must always remember to support the church by the way of Holy virtues so that God will feel comfortable within its walls as well as the hearts inside it. I believe within my statement you'll find the answer that you seek, for I love the Lord above all else."

"Well, by the Holy Spirit you possess, you have given me the answer that I seek."

"Go in peace and pray for me, Father, while remembering our Lord's word, 'Love one another as I have loved you that your joy may be full.'"

The healer's voice is next heard, "Go easy on the Father, as you must remember that he represents the authority of a higher crown. Forgive him, Father, for the prince has not been himself since his brother Liam died."

"I understand your grief, Prince Edward. I want you to know that I have a lot on my mind concerning Eridu as well."

The healer further interjects, "I believe it best if you both stay focused for the sake of the memorial service of our fallen king."

Prince Edward humbly responds, "You are right, most nobleone. As usual, I can see that you're a lantern of light filled with the wisdom of christ."

"Don't forget. It's the Holy Spirit, your majesty."

Father Jim responds, "Agreed." Then bowing his head before the prince as a subject, he turns and takes leave. On the way to the gate, a maiden meets the priest in a hooded robe. She inquires, "Excuse me. I overheard that you had concerns for Eridu, what might they be?"

"Well, who might you be, fair child?"

"I am Princess Suzy, King Ronan's mother. If you are heading towards Eridu, perhaps I could join you."

"Your highness, God is not a respecter of persons, so I must pray for a response." He silently folds his fingers and shuts his eyes for a few moments.

Princess Suzy waits in anticipation and after his eyes open, he is aglow.

"God has said to trust him, Suzy … You are to remain here."

She nods her head and says, "I will have faith."

In the woods at eve, there is prayer at Rimka's cabin and among the others who did not go with Captain James, Eagleheart announces, "Wisdom now tells me that we have to protect King Ronan. The assassins do not know whether he is in Eridu or elsewhere, so if I were to play the role of the king to draw out an assassin, perhaps we could catch one and find out who has hired them."

His uncle Eztree comments, We do not even know if these assassins were hired directly from a leader. This is far too great a risk for you to jeopardize your life."

Rimka adds, "There is no greater love that one has than laying down their life for a friend. Your love for our Lord even now exceeds your love for me. Eternal life has gripped your heart. This is good, but you must let God direct your life and not take matters unto yourself."

Her son agrees, "You're right. I do have a tendency to get impatient and not wait on the Lord's timing."

"Be at peace, my son, and you'll always have direction towards light from the warmth of our Lord's love."

"Thank you, mother." He rises from sitting at the table and goes outside to take a break from all that's been happening. While in the woods, Eagleheart notices some wild turkeys amongst the deer. He even sees a red fox. Thoughts come to him, *"How is it that all these animals can get along in the balance of nature and man cannot even get along with his own kind? For if he did, then peace would keep his soul in place and hold it for the benefit of all provinces."*

A flash of light then passes across his mind and a messenger from heaven visits him to further dispel his darkness. *"As the crown of all creation, man holds the key to how all of nature will be affected by his actions, for God has made him a steward over everything."*

"Now I see with understanding." He speaks out loud in revelation, "Mankind can upset the balance of everything by the spirits that visit his thoughts, which make him wise or dim his mind. In not seeing the outcome of what he doth, by his own hand, poor choices can cause him to stick it into an unseen dragon's mouth where by a rippling effect, all of us around the world can get bit. Herein lies the power for creation of destruction or life for us all."

A noise is heard in the barn and when Eagleheart goes to investigate, he discovers Coban to be groaning in utterances of prayer while on its earthen floor.

"Coban, what are you doing here? I thought you had left with the others."

Looking up he finishes his prayer and answers, "I have heard that you are the king's chief advisor. For him to have chosen you for this position, you must be very wise. So, I have remained to learn from you."

"I am but a mirror of our Lord's reflection of light and not all my actions are in line with Him I am sure. You might have done better if you had gone to the priests at the monastery."

"You are a humble soul that still has much to learn and I would like to share in the testimony of you doing so. For in watching your transformation from areas of darkness unto light, I feel I could learn more through your simplicity."

"Lord Jesus, let everything be done in accordance with your will as Coban has said."

Hoofbeats are heard down the road getting louder. As they approach, there is a bit of uncertainty as to whether it be friend or foe, so the two duck for cover in the barn and pray in silence 'til the Lord would have His way.

The horses approach and the voices of Captain James, Sirus, and Gray are heard along with Sage and some of his men which breaks the tension that had been felt by the two at prayer.

Sage's men offer Gray help to get down off of his horse, for he had been very stiff after being bound for so long back in the village of Ostrog.

Holding up his hand, he responds, "I'm alright, the ride seems to have loosened me up."

Eagleheart and Coban come out of the barn.

"Hi, Sirus."

"Hi, Coban," his friend responds.

Young Eagleheart gets involved, "Aren't you a sight for sore eyes. We had been wondering what happened to you and now you're here."

"You must be Eagleheart. Captain James has filled me in on our ride over, on what's been happening as of late, after Sirus was good enough to release me. I will see what we can come up with in counsel here and then go to Pine afterwards to implement a plan that would take back our kingdom."

Eagleheart suggests as he motions with his hand, "I believe we'll be more comfortable in the cabin than the barn."

"Lead the way," Councilman Gray follows right behind.

Rimka is serving Benjah, Seth, and Trig some venison stew with carrots and potatoes while Eztree sets some candles on the table in preparation of sunset. They are discovered when the door is open by the crowd of onlookers. Eagleheart leads the way before going over and giving his mother a kiss on the cheek with a kind word, "Thank you for all you do."

The remnants of the false royal hunters stand before the monastery doors as Honer knocks, using the large polished brass knocker on the door. While they wait, a horse suddenly rides up behind them carrying Duff and the other two men. Becoming inquisitive after dismounting the horse, Duff asks, "What did we miss while we were away?"

Honer answers astutely while the door is unbolted, "Only know that when you forget the beauty which lies beyond these doors, you'll recognize a full relationship behind truth with love in beholding the light of what really comes from God."

The door slowly creaks open, revealing a smiling Jerome who is pleased by the sight of the men. "Honer, how good it is to see you again and the souls you've brought with you who are so aglow."

He gives Honer a warm welcoming hug who hugs him back. Then there is a procession of hugs which follows towards each man from Jerome. Some are rigid and have trouble hugging him back, others are more responsive as some show even greater affection than Honer. He then enquires of them their names as they enter the gate.

Once inside, some remember to keep their focus on the Lord, while others become enamored with the floral garden and begin forgetting the Creator of all. Jerome sees this and uses it as an opportunity to share a lesson, "Isn't God good to have created such a variety of flowers for us to plant in honor of the fragrance of his name?" He watches as all redirect their focus to the Lord on a deeper level. "Now let us continue to be grateful for the other things which He has provided for us that you'll be seeing this day. For when the vision of God's love knocks within and is no longer containable, we learn to gently let Him out towards others. In this way, while joined to the passion of our Lord's affections, we spend time with Him rather than holding onto the forces that bite us in darkness. For when granted access to identify any desires that lead astray, we enter the gate of bonding to His divine love in our relationships with God Almighty."

Honer exclaims, "Those are my sentiments exactly!"

With a wave of his hand, Jerome leads the way, "Come now, I'm sure that the monsignor will want to hear a full report of all the latest events and about Father's Jim and Marcus."

Father Marcus makes an announcement as the wagon rolls into the center of the Nomad village before the chief of the Nomads, "Kelth, come out, I have a message that needs to be Heard from King Ronan of Eridu."

Chief Kelth comes out and sees Marcus riding next to Louisa at the reins with King Ronan holding fast to the front of the wagon while standing. After taking all this in, he signals with his hand and says, "Start the drums for the elders to come, we shall have council this eve."

Ronan nods in agreement, then the three climb down for a much needed rest after Kelth offers to tend to the horses.

Tom-tom drums are heard as they start up and the elders stop what they're doing and take notice.

One at a time, the elders make their way to the hut of meeting where a large bonfire has been lit at its center. Tahook, the medicine man, sits in his place with Tondor, his son, next to Hinsee, Kelth's son. When all the elders arrive, Kelth signals for the three who came in on the wagon. After being roused from sleep, King Ronan, Father Marcus, and Louisa soon join all who are in the hut.

Once they are seated, Kelth signals for everyone to quiet down. When it is silent, he announces that King Ronan has a message for the people. Rising up, the youth walks over by the fire before all. He then starts his proclamation, "My father, King Liam's words concerning our Savior Jesus Christ have been true. They will always be true because they are the truth which tells of the warmth of God's love you have in your hearts, bringing light for your minds to see that you love one another.

Our Savior and God, by the power of His blood, lives on forever where on the earth by His covenant with us, we are given the completed circle of eternal life. It is God who is faithful to the truth of His word and will continue to be so. His Spirit of life within our souls even now moves us into our glorified bodies in heaven. This truth will not die as the warmth of His love remains in our hearts, proving that we have been re-birthed in keeping with His promise that all may enter the circle of life by water and be divinely fed through His covenant blood.

I want you to know that the truth of God's love will never fail more than ever and even now lives on by the truth of my father, King Liam. For by his words which have been handed down through generations, they still apply as they've been given to all by God. Now I must tell you that although King Liam has died, his word's of truth still live beyond his death."

Tears appear on the cheeks of Kelth and some of the others wail aloud. Ronan holds up his hand which signifies he has more to say and when he starts to speak, Cetchem shouts for all to quiet down.

Everybody sobers up to listen more intently to King Ronan. "I am reminding you of this as there are men who will come and lie to you. They will tell you that my father, King Liam's, death brings an end to the promises of God's covenant through His

Son's flesh and blood sacrifice, yet this is untrue. It is forever real and He will not only hold your nation together, but all the provinces of Calington. This is what I've come to tell you."

The elders pass before Kelth and nod their heads. The chief then speaks for his tribe, "We understand."

Being ignored in Bumbaland, while trying to sow words of discord, the three are shunned to silence as a crowd forms around the three assassins within their land. They are followed and while fearfully leaving the village, the sound of drums intensifies the situation and losing sight of their hurried steps, a snare grabs the foot of one of them. The other two flee for fear of their lives, leaving their companion behind.

"It was almost as though they were expecting us, Spike."

"Naw! Come on, Cleave, they just have great faith."

"You're wrong, Spike. For they didn't even respond to us. It was as though everything was planned out, like we were being waited for."

"If you're right, Cleave, then we're going to have to change our strategy …"

"I'm puzzled as to how they could have known."

"Perhaps King Ronan has anticipated our move of sowing discord to split the provinces to suit our thirsts for blood, Cleave."

"If this province has been warned, the others up ahead have been warned as well. From now on, we will stay focused on killing King Ronan only or we'll end up like our friend old Blackie back there who hangs upside-down upon a tree."

Spike nods his head, "Agreed, as now that we've lost our horses by the time we arrive at the other provinces, we'll find they've been warned as well."

"How much water do you have left?"

Spike shakes one of his skins, "About a skin and a half."

"Same here. We'll make it to the Nomads okay."

"It's starting to get dark. Come on, let's find a place to make camp."

During the Night

Under the cover of clouds passing before a half moon at night, Coban, Sirus, and Sage, along with his men, set a trap to catch the contact person with the hooded mask. At the same time, Captain James, Eagleheart, and Gray make their way to the magistrates office to meet Pine.

Watching for who is going to meet the lieutenant, all eyes are on him as he stands in anticipation of meeting his contact person to give report. Well concealed and on the ready, Sage, along with his men, await the signal to take action while on their horses. A slight breeze stirs in the air by the entrance of where the road leads into the forest and over the village.

The clouds have broken and in the half moon-light, the clearing casts a brightness that causes them to emerge from out of the shadows. The captain leads the way with his hand on the handle of his sword. Once across the road, he stands in watch while Eagleheart and Gray follow across the road while nearby as he looks off in the distance.

They pass the soldier in arms and make their way to the building of the magistrate where they knock on the door. When Pine opens the door, he recognizes them and once inside, the captain is quick to follow.

"Gray, I took you for lost." The two embrace with a hug.

"I thought I was, too. If it were not for the wonderful power of our Lord to transform a heart, I would have been a goner for sure."

"I'll let the new members of King Ronan's council fill you in."

Pine asks while looking towards the hooded figure, "Why not let King Ronan?"

Lowering his hood on the robe, he responds, "I am Eagleheart, high counselor of his majesty.

"Oh, I thought you were the king himself."

"I am Eagleheart and I have a plan on exposing a secret society who has been trying to stir up strife to start a war for the purpose of taking over Eridu."

"How devious!"

"They are called 'The Ten' and will stop at nothing as they're suspected of even murdering King Liam as a part of their plan.

"It seems you have been putting a lot of pieces to this puzzle together."

"The other members of the council and I, one of which is now Captain James of the royal guard, have been putting the pieces together."

James bows his head, "At your service."

"Oh! The number ten rings a bell for some reason, only I can't quite place it yet. Oh my, if they were out to do you in Councilman Gray, it would only be a matter of time before they came after me. That's it! There were ten men who I hired as corrupt jurors that never got paid to testify on my behalf! I wonder, with their brutish manner, could they have held a grudge that has festered all this time?"

Captain James makes mention, "No matter, we have a plan which we feel would bring 'The Ten' out into the open."

Pine responds, "What do you have to say about all this, councilman?"

"First, I want you to be aware that this plan was birthed in prayer so you may know that it is from the wisdom of God."

"Understood."

"Pine, you will post a royal decree that states: Citizens of Eridu, rumors like King Ronan being kidnapped are in the air. A group of traitors called 'The Ten' carry evil ideas of plotting against all provinces for personal gain. Seeking to disrupt the peace of all of Calington is a part of their plan. Yet by the mercy of God, they shall be forgiven and receive full pardon if they disband from their actions as of now.

After everybody finishes looking over the poster, Gray continues, "I will sign it as a councilman next to the provincial seal of our provance by you, Pine. Then we shall see what will happen."

Pine questions, "But what if it doth not work?"

The Captain informs, "There is a back up plan that is underway right now."

Eagleheart remembers, "Speaking of plans, I need to get back to my mother in the woods and relieve Benjah from watching Rimka, as I am sure they could use a break from each other about now."

In the village of the Nomads, King Ronan, Louisa, and Marcus are in a guest teepee. They lounge on soft furs and are preparing to bed down for the night while making final plans for what is to happen on the morrow.

Ronan is speaking while the others listen, "… Kelth said that he will have our horses hitched to the wagon at first sun-up, Marcus."

"Good, and do not forget to make sure we have enough water, as the terrain will start to dry out on route to the Novick village."

Louisa comments, "I can look into that as I will be looking into the food supplies as well."

Ronan responds, "All right then, it's settled. We best get some rest now because we have a hard day ahead of us on the morrow."

Marcus, makes mention, "Aren't you two forgetting something?"

The two look at each other with a puzzled look.

"I am surprised about how quickly you got caught up in the busyness of the morrow after such a wonderful mass service among the Nomads. So, I see that I must pray as you two need to slow down and redirect your focus in an agreement for traveling mercies."

Back at Eridu, a lone horse approaches and stirring up the dust it clip-clops its way with an echo throughout the streets. Now out in the open, the moonlight reveals a hooded mask that is seen on the rider's head. A Short time later, the lieutenant is seen in the distance in place of Captain Paxy by the entrance to the road that leads into the woods.

Recognizing that the lieutenant is not with Gray in the village of Ostrog, he knows by intuition that something is amiss. The rider turns his horse with a kick, which causes it to go into a gallop, leaving no time to close in and trap him. Evading some riders, the chase is on throughout the streets of Eridu. Finally ducking into a shadowy alley, he jumps from his horse and lands in a wagon of hay and it rides on without the hooded man. The horse continues on, leading those who were chasing him away. Once they pass, after removing the mask, Gunta is revealed as he next hides the mask in the pile of hay.

Brushing himself off, he carefully manages to avoid being seen while moving quickly within the shadows. A gentle breeze manages to move some clouds in the night sky before the moon, and during this time under the cover of night, he maneuvers his way back to his advisors quarters at the palace going unnoticed. When the horse is subdued without its rider, it is noted that its branding is from the royal stable at the palace.

In the morning on the morrow, there are the sounds of hammer taps throughout the village as the notices are posted throughout the province at mid morn. Pine, Gray, and Captain James have banned together in prayer with a more than three fold focus which sharpens each other. They move in towards the depth of heights of God's stillness in eternity to touch His love. The windows of heaven have been opened as God's Spirit is poured out upon them. All flesh, by the Father of Lights from on high, dispells everything of darkness 'til only brilliance remains.

The finger of God's Spirit of light ignites the posters just as they are finished being hung and all eyes are drawn to them, including some of "The Ten."

The assassins are on the road towards the Nomad village when Spike realizes, "Cleave, if we were expected in Bumbaland, we'll probably be expected in all the other villages as well."

"Don't worry. We are not going to stir up trouble anymore, we're just going to get water …"

"No, look at how we're dressed. They've been warned that strangers are coming to their village, I tell you. It's possible that not only theirs, but all the villages on the road might be expecting us."

"Spike, we'll just have to go for water at night."

"At night! Do you know how long it will take us to get to the volcano?"

"What's the difference? A job is a job. The end results are always the same, Cleave."

"I guess you're right, Spike."

"I see a shady tree up ahead, we can rest during the heat of the day and conserve water now that we're moving at a slower pace."

"The Ten" have assembled and inside the secret meeting room a discussion is taking place, "… What if Pine has figured out that we are 'The Ten?'" Paps asks.

Link responds by shaking his head *no* 'til Scorch interrupts with his reply, "We are not going to win … look how things are adding up. Gunta was almost caught, the lieutenant coming to the meeting place suggests that Paxy has failed us, and Gray has signed next to Pine's seal, meaning he's been released.

Scorch hangs his head, "I did our bidding because I thought we had a better cause, but now I see that we will be stronger with King Ronan than without him. He must be restored to his proper place."

Dunge angrily responds, "There be more honor in savagery. I say we fight, right now we have the element of surprise, we could attack the magistrate ..."

Sekco gets involved, "It would never work. For after being granted an honorable pardon, posted mind you, the people would never stand behind us!"

Scorch speaks out, "There is something I have never told any of you. At the time I saw king Liam die, he had last words that stung me with a flame that I cannot put out from my thoughts, though now is not the time to share them. I for one am going after our assassins to stop them if it is not too late already. For I must try or the fire will never go out in my mind."

Gunta agrees, "I will go with you, Scorch, as I hold the coin that would release them from their obligation or they will be paid nothing."

Gordy is puzzled, "I do not fully understand, but now I want him to live or I will die in the service of putting out the sting of this flame. For without my peace of mind, there shall be no rest.

Swan throws in as well, "All that is dark is coming to light inside me with a warmth that I have never experienced before. I'm into going, too."

"Agreed," is heard from everyone else except for Dunge, who says, "I'm only coming to see what this is all about."

At the monastery, after learning about the hunters who were offered payment to start trouble, everyone is thanking God for hearing their concerns about it. The ones who have been offered coin in the hiring of them have now become the new subject of all their prayers.

Honer has his hands in the air while kneeling, "Thank you for touching the hearts of those who have offended You, my flame of life."

Bartholomew calls out from his kneeling position, "Let them now learn to always live and die for the glory of Your love."

All remains quiet for about a minute, then it is Duff who calls from the circle of hunters, "Do with us as Thine will in accordance with Thy timing and not ours. Do not allow us to be led in pride, but through the comfort of Your finger in humiliation as everything happens by Your crafting change."

Honer cries, "I now have sight! The whole world is shrouded in a darkness that allows evil spirits to fester among souls not having the Spirit of light."

Duff is quick to follow, "Why, my whole life was as dead man's bones where I have robbed the grave of others as I was looking for scraps of substance to remain alive and could not be set free 'til bending my knees to enter into eternity. Thank You, my Lord, for revealing this mystery to me."

Monsignor Bartholomew instructs, "Continue to slow down and you shall walk and talk while taking an even deeper drink of eternal life. For the deep is always calling to the deep as God's heart gets healed along with ours when we draw near. Yet, we still cannot go to Him unless we grow to Him or our pride will chase him away."

Duff questions, "How doth one overcome this?"

Bartholomew continues, "His sparks of love upon the heart shall restrain you in His light and by

His Spirit growing inside your eyes, they will open to understand that you have a friend in your Lord after tasting Him as your resurrected King. For He has the bloodline of Life that will feed you every time you partake of Him."

Father Jim is praying in the barn when Rimka comes in and notices how focused he is while kneeling before the Lord while she watches.

Rimka now has revelation on a new meaning of, "To be absent from the body is to be present with the Lord."

Jim appears not on earth, although he is here in the barn as he prays, "… I need to feel no bitter hatred when I am persecuted while walking alone with you. Your cross has now become a jeweled crown of victory for me. I know it was birthed in pain, but by the endurance of Your strength, I am able to share in Your burden which suffers love for all to the end."

Returning from being with the Lord, he is startled by Rimka's presence when noticing light coming through the open door.

"I did not mean to surprise you."

"Perhaps the Lord had you come in his timing."

"Yes, perhaps! I didn't hear you come in last night."

"I came in late. I took a few wrong turns in finding my way here and didn't want to disturb your household, so I remained in the barn."

"Has anything happened while I was away?"

"Everyone's gone off to the village except Benjah who's remained to look after me."

"Oh my! I see that I need to return to the Lord in prayer."

"You have encouraged me, Father Jim. For by the example of your faith, although all is in the movement of the night, I am sure that we shall see the sun rise on the morrow."

At another Village called the Novics, Cav, their chief, is nodding his head in response to having received news of what to expect if strangers would try to stir up strife among his people between them and Calington Castle.

He looks to the other elders on his council who in turn nod as well before looking back to King Ronan, "We have heard and will look out for these strangers."

Father Marcus observes the shadow of some nearby trees and seeing it is three O'clock, he holds up his hand to get the peoples attention. "I want each of you to know that everyone has something to contribute to our Great Father's Heart, which never ceases to love. For He has a passion towards us that draws all together to greater understand His mercy. I am going over to sit by the shade in the cool of some trees. Anyone who wishes to join me may do so." He rises from the council and sits in a suitable spot. Louisa follows close behind and as the King rises, everyone joins in.

All are curious and while still joyous from the morning mass, each one decides to worship the Father's Heart to receive His merciful love while in unity.

Giving thanks with grateful affections, praise brakes like a fountain of water that gushes forth from the love of every heart. All reach out towards receiving more of an overflowing river of God's light, treasured in mercy by the life of His blood. Their flesh wrestles against the Spirit 'til everyone fully sprouts forth, growing from out of themselves to reach another level. Plateaus are reached while climbing on His mountain in the kingdom of His peace. Yet, persevering even further, ripping through the veil of darkness to take the Creator's hand in unity, all know from His affections to whom they belong.

Tears of joy now flood every soul from the life they breathe, it washes over them from the enjoyment of taking His hand into an even greater birth as they are standing inside His presence on firm and Holy ground. This flower within His garden is both fragrant and complete. It is now time to be carried by the wind and move on as everyone is found to be content.

"The Ten" rode hard to reach the village of Ostrog, but will they find them there or is this to be a first destination in tracking the assassins down?

This question weighed heavy on their minds as they journeyed on to seek answers from the village. Afterward, meeting with Scorch and Gordy who remained to watch the horses at the well not far from the edge of the road, everyone's findings are discussed.

At first it was believed that they hadn't come this far when their unity was observed, but after hearing about how a royal guard restored all to order in the light of truth, "The Ten" knew that they had passed by this way.

After a greater exchange of information taking place between them, Gunta further enquires among his men, "Was everyone as unsuccessful as me?"

While exchanging looks, Swan volunteers, "I found out that they were here and have gone."

Gunta presses him, "Did you find out what direction they were heading?"

"I asked if there were any strangers in their village recently. I then heard tale of a few and when I inquired more deeply describing how they were dressed, I heard that the ones we seek headed out in the direction of the monastery."

"They never would've stopped at the monastery, so we must look for them in the lands beyond. Let us be off!"

All mount up and ride on 'til passing the monastery before encountering Bumbaland where to their surprise they behold Blackie standing on the side of the road where they would have entered, holding the reins of three horses. He then responds, "Now I know why I am standing here."

Gunta speaks for himself and the others, "Yes, we have met the one who has died and yet lives in our hearts with fire, too."

Dunge asks, "Where are Cleve and Spike?"

"I don't know. I was only told to bring their horses. For after meeting Him and knowing the passion of our Great One, an angel of The Lord appeared before King Bumba and I when we were praying together. He was told to release me from the camp and bring me here. Standing here on the freedom of this road, I have stood only moments before you've arrived. I now have received a greater understanding of how God releases from within."

Dunge answers with surprise, "Now I've heard and seen everything that I've been looking for. I would like to meet this God that you know so well. For you are aglow with the change of answers that I seek."

Gunta suggests, "Let us continue on and perhaps you will find the answers you are looking for."

Caught

The sun begins its descent as the men dismount and start to gather wood for a fire. It gradually builds to roaring flames while adding sticks.

After setting their blankets, they take eat of some salted strips of pork as a half moon begins to appear at dusk. At nightfall, "The Ten" plus one start to settle in for the night.

We find Cleave and Spike stepping into the moonlight and coming out of the shadows from the tree-line, their scent is now exposed upon the breeze. While going for water, a lookout, who is posted for hunting wild animals that come at times by night, picks up on their scent. Seeing them, he is swift to awaken others.

Having quietly filled their water skins while facing the water, when they rise and turn, the assassins realize that they've not gone unnoticed. Many eyes are upon them from only a few feet away.

Kelth passes through them with his walking staff in hand and the crowd makes way for him. Looking at the assassins he says, "Come be our guests."

With waterskins in hand, they follow the chief into the crowd which surrounds them and they follow close behind.

He stops before his tent where sitting before it, he motions with his hand for them to sit as well, laying his staff to the ground. Young maidens come and sit next to them and the chief then instructs, "They will tend to your needs while you become accustomed to our ways." He motions with his hand again, "This is Running Deer and this is Little Feet."

Cleave's and Spike's eyes open wide beholding their beauty and Kelth immediately discerns their lustful thoughts.

kelth catches their attention and explains, "The desires of your lustful hearts imprison you by wanting their flesh without understanding their souls. Just as your lust for riches has given you a thirst for blood that can never be satisfied by the compulsion that drives you. For when wanting something more that someone else has, it causes you to take your eyes off of God who is able to provide. What you desire will not meet your need as you seek a path that has no light."

The two pull their knives and hold them to the throats of the young maidens, Cleave speaks for them both, "We'll be leaving your camp now and don't try to stop us."

"You are not our captives, so why would I try to stop you?"

Cleave responds angrily, "You're lying!"

"If I were to lie, I would be in the prison that I sought to release you from. For those who choose to do evil over good are trapped in a darkness that doth not allow one to see light."

"We are not captive to anyone as we are free!"

"Our people do not consider themselves held captive because our thoughts are not limited to visions of the dark. There is light as we walk in the light."

Spike lowers his knife, "What is this light you speak of?"

"It is the light which draws one to be satisfied while having much with only a little. As when alive, you can see what you have beyond the dark. For by its Spirit you can breathe the breath that offers only life and have sight of a direction that will lead you into an eternity filled with life."

Cleave lowers his knife as well, "With those words, I can tell you do not lie, I want to hear more."

"I was once chief of my tribe without being chief over myself. For I was once nobody until the somebody of Jesus Christ, the Son of the living God, discovered me in His love. He brought light to my path and I want you to know that His love is still available for you, too."

Cleave questions, "I do not understand."

"Has the way you've been living your life truly left you satisfied?"

Cleave quiets himself and after a few moments, he says, "I am listening."

"I was like a dark branch, cut off from The Great Father's vine of light as pressures from darkness gripped me with spirits 'til rejoined by the mercy of the blood of His Son, sacrificed to bring all unto eternal life."

Spike suddenly becomes weary and starts to doze off while his partner presses on to focus intently. "I want to see beyond the darkness and know the warmth of our great Fathers love, which joins one to His light of what you call eternal life. For you have said, all are included by the mercy of His blood, which lives beyond every single sacrifice."

"I see you at the door. Now all that is necessary is for you to open the gate to your heart that His truth knocks with. For by the name of Jesus Christ, you can invite Him in and have light."

Cleave shouts, "Jesus Christ, I open my heart to you!"

Spike is suddenly awakened and asks, "Cleave, what has happened?"

"I have received a breath that breathes the breath which fills with eternal life. It has entered through the living blood of Jesus Christ, Son of God and sacrifice."

"Cleave, it is you, but it is not you."

"It's okay. Darkness has left me. Now I am filled with a light that gives clarity to a life with sight. For I can see into the forever and know the freshness that it brings. I am too grateful of His love to kill anymore. For I see that a part of Him lives within every man, giving all a chance to love by light in place of hate throughout the darkness we are in."

Spike gets frightened, "I'm getting out of here."

Running away from them he heads towards the woods as Cleave calls out, "Wait, don't go!"

Kelth is quick to tell him, "Do not be conflicted, it is just not his time."

Cleave is quick to respond, "I will go after Him."

"Do you not know that he'll be all right by what has happened to you? He flees from the light that's in you that he doth not understand. Now is the time to call on the Spirit Father of all lights who is in you. For it shall take God's power to ignite his soul with the vision you now have. This will be more effective than anything you have to say. So you are better off telling it to your new Lord, who has bought you from out of the dark by your prayer."

"I still feel like there is something I can do."

"The words that I spoke to you are Spirit and they have brought you life by the light of truth. Know you not that you have been redeemed by the warmth of God's love out of darkness and must remember that this is only something which God can do as you didn't make yourself. For if you could fasten on wings and fly then you'd be the Great Father Himself. Let him go. For although he has left our village, the truth of God's presence will be with him no matter where he goes."

"I see what you're saying, so I will remain with you and talk to the Father of lights through the door of Christ's blood through the rest of this night."

When the sun awakens there's a chill in the air from the cool of morn. "The Ten" emerge from their blankets, along with Blackie. All walk to warm themselves and as the dawn shares more light, they pack and tend to the horses. A song of praise breaks forth from Blackie who notices some birds fly over the mountains and this encourages the others to join in while they go about their business: "I've seen your birds, they're way up high. I've seen the mountains reach the sky, but no one touches me inside like you do, Lord. It is Your song that's in my heart. I should have known You from the start, Your start which caused my mind to see within Your star. And now my destination set, beyond the veil that's in the night, for I am guided by your light to know your love."

Dunge interjects, "Hallelujah! That's my God," and joins in.

They repeat the song 'til they are well settled in their faith and are ready to move on.

The singing fades as they mount up, but not to the song that satisfies a soul as the presence of God's hand continues to hold their affections.

Back on the open road, Dunge fully recognizes more of the gentleness that has touched his heart and knows that he now breathes the breath of life as well. They next set out for the village of the Nomads.

Kelth is up, walking staff in hand, chanting a sweet melody with a dance to The Great One and Lord over creation while focusing his mind to see beyond the dim and into the brilliance of God's light. The dawn has awakened to pierce the dark veil of night. He is now ready to spend another day in eternity where darkness shall not overtake the presence of God's life.

Cleave is up as well and having observed the chief, he questions him when he sits by the entrance of his lodge with staff in hand, "What was the purpose of your chant?"

He motions with his hand, "Come! Sit by me and I will tell you of the dance of The Great Spirit of light."

Sitting next to Kelth, he looks over at the chief and gives him his attention, "I am ready."

"Take my staff in hand and draw a circle in the sand."

Rising, he takes the staff in hand from Kelth and draws a circle near them.

Kelth states, "This is the soul of the earth."

Cleave nods his head and awaits further instruction.

"Now collect sticks and scatter them around the circle."

Taking up some kindling wood, he doth as he is asked until it is completely surrounded.

"Just as our earth is surrounded by darkness, so do invisible forces press in on our souls from what is not seen in dark light, too. These sticks are as such."

The walking stick drops to the ground at the realization of what has been said.

"Pick up my staff and retrieve some black ash from the fire pit on one of its ends. Then return it to me and I will tell you more."

Cleave is quick to pick up the pole and doth what he's been told. Then he eagerly looks on in the chief's direction.

"Now I want you to draw a small circle within the larger circle with a line next to it off to one side of the larger original one. Use the end of my stick without the ash. Good! Now place the end of the staff in the small space on the other side of the line which cuts through the big circle. Inside the smaller space, you must turn my staff around and press until there is a dark small spot within it."

The old assassin looks curiously on with lots of questions and waits for further teaching to get his answers.

"Now I want you to understand that all of creation testifies of the Creator and His kingdom. So you must look to how the sun, earth, and moon relate to each other in what you have drawn in the circle of their dance. For this is where the answer that you seek will come to sight. Then you shall understand a part of the vision of creation when looking to the night sky."

Finished, Cleave looks on and waits.

"Take your knife out and score the black spot with the thin edge of the blade. Each time you do this, the spot will narrow. Draw a line next to where you cut the circle 'til it expands past the drawing of the wider one. Use the flat part of the blade and cross the larger circle with more lines. Once moved over, the lines will fill the space between them and cover over the smaller dark circle and both will be filled in, leaving the original circle 'til reaching its edge."

While he is working, Cleave hesitates and tries to figure out what he is doing.

The chief then reminds him, "Remember, I want you to do this 'til both the small dark spotted circle within the larger circle that is cut will gradually disappear into the sand from inside the original one as well."

When he finishes what the chief has told him, he looks on again.

Kelth then asks, "Do you know what I am trying to show you?"

Cleave just stands and shakes his head without a clue.

"Take your knife and from out of the edge of the original circle, I want you to clear a path, line upon line, until there is a clear path through the sticks. Then I want you to remove the sticks 'til they're completely gone."

He continues and when he's done looks up again.

"Now take the staff and make larger circles around the original one until you reach where I sit and hand my staff back to me."

His new student still looks on questionably.

"Still don't understand, do you?"

Cleave shakes his head again.

"My staff that you handed me is a symbol of authority like God's creating hand. The outer circles have reached beyond the original space of a soul that we've first started out with. This is how we grow when we come to understand that drawing nearer to the deep comes from the love of our Lord's embrace.

What you have seen is what happens between the seasons of sun and moon as they pass each other in shadows with the earth in between. How they relate to each other is an example of how we press through all darkness that shifts from a dark new moon to a full one of light in seasons of seeking the truth. Now know from this time forth that there are spirits that live within shadows when calling upon God as He is the Father of all light that we pray to.

Everything in creation is a part of the nature of His laws and they convey a message to all men by them. We go through growth by the order of this dance as God transforms us from darkness unto light. He has set all things together within the order of its place. He doth not go against His law, but if man so chooses to stray in his ways, a conscience can be violated 'til one is left in the dark. Minds are left in lunacy without any light, for when man breaks God's law, He cannot feed Him the essence of His truth and eventually all turns to night."

Cleave shouts out, "Praise God - I understand! Our darkness leaves our minds when we comprehend God's love as all that is dark gets cast out in the light of knowing Him." The sound of many horses on the approach next eclipses their thoughts.

The two look over and see "The Ten" arriving through the bustling village as many are awake. Before anyone can move … It is then realized that they're carrying a tune of worship towards the Great One Himself: "There's a land called paradise where heavens quires sing. There's a land called paradise where Christ is Lord and King. Can you skip like a calf, laugh like a mule, come on you faithful, rejoice in all your youth? There's a land called paradise where heavens choirs sing. There's a land called paradise where Christ is Lord and King."

Cleave looks towards Kelth who says, "I would say that they're friends."

The old assassin sees who's riding next to Gunta his old boss. Then realizing that he's alive as they finish their song, he shouts, "Blackie!"

He in turn exchanges a glance with Cleave and as he acknowledges him, the truth bears witness of itself in each other's eyes. Both say to one another at the same time as they look on, "You're alive!"

The Novic Village

Spike has been walking on the road during the night and into the morning. He has shed off one of three waterskins along the way and now exhausted during travel, he lifts his head on hearing someone singing nearby. Following the tune of, "Let not thine heart be troubled, nor let it be afraid. Let not thine heart be troubled, for on my cross it was paid. You crown-nth us with tender mercies and loving kindness upon our heads. Let not thine heart be troubled, nor let it be afraid. Let not thine heart be troubled, for on my cross it was paid."

He becomes intrigued by the words while walking and finds himself entering the village of the Novics. When the brave finishes his task, Spike approaches as he rises and starts to walk away carrying a bundle of sticks for firewood. "Pardons, but what was that song you were singing about?"

"About a man I could not follow 'til by His Spirit, I was discovered by Him as Christ. He has been transforming me into the image of His name, Jesus, which I am becoming more grateful for every day."

"I do not understand."

"I am outgrowing who I was and entering into a newer and better nature in each stage of my growing life. For now, becoming a part of the essence of Christ, I live, breathe, and move in my being as his bride. Every time He enters into me, I am birthed to further grow in height and depth while we are one." The brave puts down his bundle by the fire pit where they are noticed by others who begin to pray for the visitor.

Then while he is returning for more sticks, Spike steps in front of him and asks, "What else can you tell me?" All at once, he realizes that the brave's eyes look just like Cleave's, his partner who he just fled from.

"I am known as Thorn. Now I believe it is time to know the name of the one who questions me."

He answers apprehensively, "I am Spike."

"Spike, I as Thorn am glad to meet you. I can see that we are both sharp and believe that it was no accident we have met."

Cleave's hunger for Thorn's words override his uneasy feelings, "You have my ear, Thorn."

"Like a bee pollinating a flower, I have been stilled by His gentle wind for Him to satisfy me from deep within. Every time He enters, I grow a little more in truth, which matures me to grow out of the dark soil of my youth. I am now rooted and grounded in His love, which sparks His light from beyond above."

"I want what you have."

"I have started out as a seed of faith from learning how to listen to what all creation has to say. You cannot wear what I am wearing until taught to grow in what I know. Yet God's seed of truth is available to grow when planted deeply inside a heart as the Creator of creation wants to clothe you as his bride, too. For as a jewel, you've been pressed in the pressures of the dark that you might be set upon His setting to sparkle in His light. Willful wants of flesh will block you from the Spirit of all light as darkness desires to hold you for its own. So the decision is yours as our God of love doth not force Himself on anyone." Thorn returns to tending to his work of gathering up more sticks and begins to hum a joyful tune.

"Alright! I am tired of the life I have. For it is a stale existence next to yours."

"His name is Jesus. Call out to Him with all your heart until He touches and enters it with his seed. Then every creation will speak and guide you to His blood that lives forever. So, if you listen to the Spirit that leads to find the circle of His substance of life, you will truly discover what it is to be alive."

Spike cries out, "Help me!" as he falls to his knees and begins to weep while saying, "Help me!" again.

"The Ten" from the road are nearby. His cry is heard by Cleave and Blackie, who recognize Spike's voice.

Looking at each other, they cry out, "Spike is in trouble!"

Veering from the others, they take off towards the direction of where his cry was heard. Then while riding, it is noticed "The Ten" are with them from the sounds of their horses. Upon arrival, they all find Spike to be on his knees sobbing. Yet soon it is realized that he is not sorrowful as he is crying tears of Joy as they hear him saying, "Thank you, Jesus. Thank you, Jesus."

Upon the arrival of the others, Thorn's bundle falls to the ground. All of the sticks that he was gathering are scattered due to his anticipation of trouble. Though when he notices that the truth bears witness of itself while making eye contact with them, Thorn knows that he is in good company and he shouts, "This is a cause for celebration!"

At Calington court, a discussion is taking place between Prince Edward and his niece, Princess Suzy. "… Suzy, I want to support your son as my desire is for us to go to Eridu. I have not forgotten that Ronan is my beloved nephew, but as my mind grieves about my brother, it weighs heavily on me and causes it to become hard for me to focus clearly.

The timing will be right when my peace fully rests on the Lord's shoulders again. Otherwise, I'd be trusting in myself and not relying on Him.

Suzy speaks with an understanding tone in her response, "I understand what you're saying, but wouldn't a visit with your nephew help bring some cheer and help you in your healing?"

"I am rent like a garment and only the love of our Great One can mend the hurt that I feel for me to heal as he knows my sufferings by the cross he bore."

"How do you know He didn't send me to help? Perhaps seeing Ronan would help sooth the hurts you feel where you would better heal. For just as you have said, 'We are not to take matters into our own hands, but trust in God,' Isn't this something that you might be doing?"

"You are right. I have been selfish, for in hardening my heart in pride, the warmth of God's love has grown cold like steel, replacing the warmth of light which was there. Yet now I realize that I've left our Lord's side. We shall start out for Eridu on the morrow, for I could do with a change of scenery."

The Novic tribe dances circling around a large stationary cross at the center of the village. They are in celebration of their guests who are soon to be baptized. Desiring the full redemption of being planted into God's Kingdom has come.

Now being led by His Spirit to do so, "The Ten" along with Cleave, Blackie, and Spike watch joyous expressions as they pass before them in tribal dance while chanting sweet spiritual melodies of praise. Finally filled with the Holy Spirit, a vision of light tells Cav, their leader, that it is time for an increase in the unity of God.

Cav stops his dance with a stable firm stance and raising his hands, he signals for the visitors to rise and follow as well.

After Cav goes down to the lake, everyone else follows him one at a time. Each man stands before this one who has learned to humble himself before the tribe.

Immersing them in the name of the Father, Son of creation of all things by the word of His image, alive through His living flesh and blood, everything is now discovered refashioned by being recreated.

His perpetual lineage of resurrection breaks the seal of darkness and opens the door to the circle of truth which applies knowledge to their lives in the form of wisdom. All are reunited within the existence of being held together by His Spirit of light that lives in truth. The presence of God's heavenly kingdom will now guide their way home.

The Holy Spirit, line upon line, orchestrates the essence of growth as pure. It is the reference to the character of truth and completely weaves in hope to all. For as the deep calls unto the deep in a love that grants understanding to partake in the practice of the circle of life, all return fond affection to God.

Clarity comes to mind forever to everyone while walking hand in hand within His light, for when all is brilliant, there is only a direction for sight.

Full restoration begins inside the circle that lives throughout every creation, which gives it a power to bring forth life. Our Lord offers a living blood to now be resurrected in a testimony of where darkness has now been defeated and the bloodline which we live in that dies can end at last.

Being brought into His world, the earth only disappears from thought when we no longer belong to the dimness of the dark. All grows through each stage of completion to leave it 'til ripe on the vine. Christ plants His living seed in others next to reproduce after His own regenerative kind.

Eyes are alighted with smiles that grin from ear to ear as all come out of the water, joining everyone who now dances around the cross with movements and melodies of praise with heartstrings of harps that are filled with life in their songs.

The aroma of the chants of music are carried loudly enough by the wind for the passersby to overhear in the wagon inwhich they ride. Louisa is at the reins when Marcus requests for her to stop before next encouraging her to head in the direction of the music.

Ronan protests, "But we were on our way back to Eridu. You knowing that I was told by a dream to return immediately, this presses against all else."

Marcus responds, "Did you not say that your dream was like music to your ears?"

"That was just a figure of speech."

"No, you prophesied and I shall prove it to you my king. Louisa, continue on to the village of the Novic's as I feel in The Spirit that some answers await us there."

"As your king, I command you to not stop at the Novic Village …"

The wagon pulls out of sight off the trail as it disappears into the woods to the sound of Ronan protesting, "… What are you doing?"

"I tried to hold to the road, your majesty, but our beasts of burden seems to have minds of their own."

At the cross, the celebration of song and dance continues. The wagon's stopping stirs up a cloud of dust from the road that the wind carries into the faces of some of those who dance. When they stop and go for water, they notice the wagon. Thorn, who is among them, proclaims, "King Ronan has returned once more with the priest! We shall have another mass."

The dancing stops and the songs die down to a quiet fire within their hearts. Marcus then notices the countenances of everyone there, including those who they earlier met on the road back in Eridu. Marcus nods in acknowledgment of their hunger for the Lord. He then suggests to Ronan, "Would those be the three faces that you saw in your dream last night?"

Ronan suddenly cries out from the wagon before the Lord to all after sensing a change in the countenance of the three that they had met on the road earlier, "Lord, I'm scared, for I have become anxious, causing me to almost miss this blessing.

Deliver me from my foes which try to stumble me as there are spirits that almost gained entrance into my soul by looking away from your affections towards me, my love. For flesh has caused me to let down my guard and war against Your Spirit, yet another time. Now I ask You to hold all my focus and change me by Your hand. Take me into the essence of your nature and continue to transform me through Your flesh and blood in the covenant I am keeping with you. Craft me by Your Spirit and I will be changed into a worthy vessel that shall always contain your essence while in Your service. Amen."

Gunta, the leader of "The Ten," shouts out, "Long live King Ronan, the just!"

Everyone else joins in 'til their shout becomes a single voice, "Long live King Ronan! Long live King Ronan!"

When things quiet down, Cav becomes inquisitive and approaches his majesty, "I thought I overheard Marcus mention a dream. What was it about?"

A surprised king speaks out, "I believe it would be better if I told everybody," Ronan next stands before the cross, "People of Novic, it was mentioned to me that some of you heard that I had a dream. From what I'm seeing here, I believe it was a vision that's coming to pass. I share this to further encourage your faith. For when we stopped for a rest in the valley of the dead, I now realize that falling into a vision, I did not sleep. What I saw were three men who joined with me in prayer, coming out from shadows into light. Then I heard a voice saying it was safe for me to return to Eridu, which came from the light. Based on this, I turned back towards my province and was encouraged by Marcus, my riding companion to stop. Yet, I did not listen because I took on entitlements as a king which would have rolled the world back on my shoulders. Although, God in His mercy did not allow this to happen. For now, here we stand stopped before you."

His riding companion and priest speaks up, "Do you recognize any of the faces that you saw in your vision here?"

The king looks around and before long, he picks out the three old assassins who are standing among the tribe and the others, pointing them out.

Marcus responds, "These were the three men who spoke to us while you were under the blanket in the Tall Hills, on the road in the back of the wagon among the supplies. Now listen to what they have to say and the blessing of how God has changed their countenance."

Blackie testifies,"Using wisdom copied from men, I tried to survive while hate filled my heart in a world that was harsh. Yet, God's wisdom opened the door for His love to come in and let me out of this world by His truth which still lives to replace all abuse. For my mind was divided 'til He sat on my throne to thaw the flesh around my heart which now feels affection."

Spike shares as well, "When I sought to satisfy my desires that were dark and without sight, I was heading in the wrong direction while on earth, but once I stepped into heaven, I became alive and satisfied to no longer stumble by being insane. For choosing to practice what I did not understand left me to blame. Yes, God healed my mind and now I focus on Him inside as my torments have been removed."

Cleave rejoices as well, "My mind and heart were eclipsed by a darkness that had me in knots 'til His light of truth came to change my stature of height. God's love now fills me as I relate to Him with sight, for once I was missing Him and did not know myself.

The King encourages, "If God be for us, then what manner of spirit dragon can stand against us?"

On the Road

In the throne room at the castle, the healer and Prince Edward are holding private counsel on how a visit to Eridu should be handled, "… Majesty, if you were to ride into the province with an army in a show of force to support Ronan due to the unrest there, it might be taken as an invasion among their people. For, as of right now, things are rather delicate."

"Your counsel holds true once again. For as my family is involved, my emotions are running high. So, what would you recommend I do when visiting Eridu as my judgement is still off?"

The healer responds, "Take out the army of Calington, only leave them outside of the village and enter with your envoy of royal guard along with messengers alone this way if there is any trouble, you can send a dispatch for the army to come at once if need be."

Prince Edward next motions for a messenger to come. He comes over and stands quietly before and awaits instruction. "Send for the captain of my royal guard."

The healer rises, "If I might pardon myself, mass starts in twenty minutes and I feel a need for some extra time of reflection this day."

"For some reason, I feel led to attend church at Eridu later today, though while you're before the altar, pray that our venture goes well."

The healer smiles, "It's always an honor to bring requests before our Father as He delights in hearing the voices of His children when they call."

Prince Edward smiles, "Your encouragement has peeled back my burden already as you have reminded me that He has the power to lift them."

Eagleheart is in the barn hitching up a second horse to the wagon when his mother comes in finely dressed. "I'll put the feed bags on em so you can get ready." Rimka's son then exits the barn leaving her to tend to the horses. She opens the mouth of a half-empty sack of oats and uses a small bowl to poor two scoops in each feedbag before placing them on each horse.

Finished buttoning his shirt while in the cabin, Eagleheart sits in a ready chair at the kitchen table. Pulling on his boots over a clean pair of pants, now well dressed, he rises, grabs his jacket, and after walking out the door, he puts it on while going to the barn. Once through the barn door, he sees his mom removing a final feedbag from off of the second horse and soon after helps her in the wagon.

Swinging open the large barn doors, Rimka drives out the wagon. Closing them, Eagleheart climbs on and they start a slow ride towards the village as not to stir up the dust.

Rimka asks while facing the road at the reigns, "How come we're going to town so early when church isn't until 4 o'clock?"

"I wanted you to meet Pine, the magistrate. He has quite a testimony … and you might find him rather interesting."

"Are you trying to fix me up?"

"How can you say that when you've taught me that it is God who is the revealer of mysteries?"

Rimka has a questionable look, "I'm sure if Father Jim hadn't left so early, he would probably be riding along side in agreement."

In the magistrates office, Pine, Gray, and Captain James are having a discussion about the posters effectiveness that have been put up throughout the village. "… Well, things seem pretty quiet." says the magistrate.

James responds, "That could be good or bad, Pine."

Gray enquires, "How so?"

"They could have heeded our warning and disbanded or might be laying low while scheming another plan."

Pine becomes concerned, "That would not be good."

The captain suggests, "We shall remain calm as it is written in the *Book of Life* that, 'Those who wait upon the Lord shall renew their strength.' I now recall how a change in Eagleheart's character grew him into the maturity of his new name."

Pine smiles and says, "You cause me to remember how my character was changed when my mind was ruled in a pact with lies 'till the light of God came in."

Captain James shakes his head, "I see a difference between you and Eagleheart."

Gray curiously asks, "How so?"

"Your conversion was more like a solar eclipse whereas the youths more like a complete lunar cycle coming into the light of a full moon."

Gray replies, "I'm sure there is a variation of combinations as well."

Pine's eyes become wide, "Thank God for the wisdom of His mercy."

The captain becomes soldier-like rather suddenly, "While we're waiting, perhaps we should seek out the ten men who were at court under your direction when things were rather dark for you, Pine."

All at once the front door creaks open and in walks Cunna. Pine becomes elated while sitting at the bench, he is the first to see their old leader enter. The others turn and smile as well.

Cunna smiles back in response, "That's quite a greeting, I'm happy to see everyone, too."

Pine looks on in a light hearted manner, "You may approach the bench."

"I'd say, with King Ronan missing and those posters about with your endorsement, I do not need permission to approach." Now standing before them, he enquires, "How did this turn of events come to pass?"

Gray responds in front of everyone spread out around the courtroom as they look on, "I believe the ten jurors who were at the trial are in league with the dark spirit that came out of pine when joining the kingdom of light."

"Then why not watch them and see what lay behind their actions?" suggests Cunna.

Pine raises his hand while shaking his head, "That's what we were doing when you came in."

"Easy there, this should be taken as a confor-mation. We have enough dragon spirits around here without inviting more."

"I completely agree as I know how dark and deceptive the spiritual world can be."

Sage eagerly volunteers, "Rest assured, my men could cover tracking down the ten as the light they now bear shall easily discover their darkness."

Gray gets involved again, "Speaking of the spiritual world, after observers of the ten jurors are sent forth, you could attend church with us later and tell us some of your missionary experiences."

"Let us see what the Lord will do as it might not be what He has in mind." Cunna then turns to the others and recognizes them to be Sons of Ishmael and asks while pointing his finger to each, "You would be?"

"Coban."

"And you would be?"

He is apprehensive, but finally says his name, "Sirus."

"No need for worry as I know of your concerns. Though, we had a fierce hatred in battles as enemies of war, now we are brothers in eternal life as citizens of heaven." Then extending his hand towards each, they shake as warm smiles break forth.

Passing through the Tall Hills, just past the mountains of Zantee, the skin of a large mountain lion can be seen in the back of the wagon as it lays out to dry. Louisa drives the horses while Marcus sits in the middle and Scorch rides by Ronan's side from on his horse. The king smiles on at him while exchanging words, "Scorch, I want you to know that from now on, you shall be my personal bodyguard."

He questions himself with an uncomfortable look and then answers, "I am not worthy of such an honor."

"Not worthy? Anyone who would risk his life to save me from the jaws of a lion with their bear hands, like you did, is more than worthy. I don't know if I would have saved me like you did. Diving off your horse and snatching the jaws of death that were upon me. If you are not a God send then I don't know what is."

Marcus becomes involved, "Majesty, gratitude is one thing, but you are to be sure that it enhances and doth not distract you from your relationship with God. For aren't you neglecting the free will that God has allowed you by forcing him to serve?"

"You're right, Marcus, love doth not force. What say you, Scorch?"

"I need time to consider. Although after I pray, the Lord shall instruct me on what He would have me to do."

Now nearing the place where king Liam has died on the road just north of Liam's pass, Prince Edward stops his horse and begins to weep on seeing where fresh soil has been lain upon the grond. Next, holding up his hand, he signals for everyone else to stop as well. The royal guard brings a small wagon being pulled by a donkey with a large stone. At a closer look, the engraving chiseled out on the stone reads, "Here rests the body of King Liam, ruler and faithful servant to, 'The Christ,' of all lands."

After the stone is set, homage is paid in a moment of silence to where King Liam's body has been laid. When the tears dry on his brother's face, he makes a proclamation: "We hang our heads low at this time as my brother King Liam's shadow hangs over us. Yet do not be discouraged, for the memory of his love shall remain with us forever and bring light back into our lives."

Suzy is rather delicate in what she says, "My father knew more than most would care to know. For in his closeness to God, he felt our Lord's pain. He identified with the sufferings of something much worse than the cross he bore for us all, too. I have seen it in his eyes, how Liam has felt the rejection of God's love from his children of whom he has created for affections of heart. So now let his loss, tearing at our stitch work between thoughts and emotions, be a comfort in the essence of God's character towards us. For He is found to know all our infirmities through His Son, Jesus Christ."

"Let us now cry out and let the Lord begin to fill in our tears in the mending of our hearts."

Back at the court of the magistrate, Sage and his men open the door to discover Rimka and Eagleheart, who step aside to let them out before entering.

Captain James calls out, "Ah! Rimka, Eagleheart, come, there's someone I want you to meet." Turning to Cunna as they come forward, "These are the other members of King Ronan's council."

Cunna looks on their countenances, "I can tell through your Relationship with the Great One that He loves others into His kingdom by the truth they bear."

Rimka responds, "And I can see that you bear the truth, which holds to bear witness with ours."

"Amen!" says Eagleheart as the magistrate catches his eye while looking to his mother. "Oh, mom, this is Pine our magistrate."

"My son believes that we should talk. What are your feelings on the matter?"

"All in God's timing."

"I like that. Very well then, let us see if a bud will bloom on the branch of our Lord's vine."

The royal envoy from Calington Castle arrives in the village of Eridu outside the office of the magistrate. Prince Edward instructs his personal guards to wait with the horses and instructs his messenger what to do if there is any trouble. Him and the princess enter in. Once inside, they approach the bench with all looking on.

Pine acknowledges Suzy right away, "Princess Suzy, how good of you to come."

"Anything that concerns our son concerns me, too."

"It has been a lifetime ago for me. Perhaps after all is said and done, it will be a time of healing for everyone."

Rimka becomes involved, "Although there is quite a difference in age between you, I see that you two know each other rather well."

Pine makes an unusual statement, "It is true, we have known each other, but we really never knew each other.

Rimka responds, "I am from another land and do not know your story."

"When I lived in darkness, I made some mistakes as I practiced what I did not understand and while in this light of truth, I was not myself. For, I knew not the Christ of light and love." He then looks to the princess, "When I met you while in darkness, Suzy, I never knew your love."

Rimka then responds to Suzy, "I see that you still carry scars that bear much pain, Princess."

"It is true, I still hurt as my heart aches within me towards a man I now see I never knew. Perhaps this man, I can now forgive. For in realizing that this man I have never known means me no harm. By the grace of God, I see that the old man is dead in Christ and the new man is alive through him as well. I can no longer be angry with him as God has forgiven me for my sins just like him."

Pine becomes elated, "Wonderful, I have prayed for this moment a long time as I have bore a wound from the hurt that I've caused you and now I am healed, too. Thank you for your help in this matter, Rimka.

"My help? I did nothing but quiet myself in loves embrace while slowing down before the Lord. For outside of the motion of this world's darkness, it was revealed to me that it takes stillness of mind to have focus within the kingdom of the light of God."

All look on in the room in a sense of awe as she continues, "I now rest with God in the silent realm, which gives all a walk of life inside an eternity of sight. He is the way, the truth, and when He reveals His mysteries in time, it enhances our growth within a soundness in every stage of eternal life."

Pine makes a statement to help Him better focus on what is being said, "I see that you've been studying the laws of nature, which testify of the Creator through creation. I see that your relationship with God has blossomed from the solitude of your stay in the woods."

"Man's knowledge must be out of the way to gain wisdom from God. For a singleness of thought allows us to see that there's a great dividing noise in a double mindedness that can intrude when other ideas are around. I remember when I first got rooted and grounded in the love of Christ, how mixed ideas sparked confusion and blocked the stability to plant His seed, preventing completion to grow into the purity of still and eternal light."

Suzy confirms what is being said, "The sounds of others do distract as this is a current problem that faces not only I but us all."

"I was still dim 'til pressing through to take the hand of my Redeemer, too. As leaving the dark, I entered into a brilliance that now knows His mind. Yes, by trusting, He gave me strength to meet Him beyond the veil, I have taken His hand.”

Eagleheart speaks with a grateful heart, “That's my momma!”

Captain James becomes involved as he points, “Sorry to interrupt, but according to the sun shining on that window, it is time to go to church.”

Wisdom

The gathering house that invites God's presence to tabernacle with His children has been built at the center of the village of Eridu.

Now having the focus of the people, they meander their way towards its entrance to usher in another new week of being grateful to their King of all kings who provides for them. Prince Edward and his envoy along with all those who were at the Court of the magistrate join in the line for those who lack the soundmind of peace. This is to prepare their hearts through the gate of all conscious light within a mind. For there can be no corruption allowed to enter back in that would hinder God's purity from entering a heart by His light. What lives in darkness blocks the strength of joy, unsettles love, and robs the firm foundation of peace by troubling thoughts 'til day turns vision night.

An eclipsed soul must not receive the Holy Host divine, for it can sever a relationship by spewing the lukewarm from God. Confessing places where all fall short of honor having missed the rest of being planted in Him, we repent from what is called sin. Now Christ is able to absolve each man before His ear when spoken out in humility's light. For He's able to cleanse us of every unrighteousness with this preparation that we enter His presence which fills from within. He desires to meet with everyone of His children in this way. However, some lack understanding Him and shrink away from the blessing of commingling in Eucharistic adoration with Him.

King Ronan, Louisa, Marcus and "The Ten" arrive at the church with those who are no longer assassins and all are noticed. Pine says to Captain James, Gray, and Cunna, "Look, it is 'The Ten' with assassins among them, this could mean double trouble."

Gray comments, "No! See there. King Ronan and Marcus are with them, perhaps everything is okay."

Cunna adds, "Unless there is a threat upon their heads."

Princess Suzy comments as well, "No, my son smiles from within and is filled with the light of joy. If there was any trouble, I would know it. Let me get his attention to satisfy that skeptical look on your face, Cunna."

"Go right ahead."

Rimka waves her arm, "Ronan, over here!"

Upon seeing his mother, Ronan calls back, "Ma, come sit with us!"

"Why not sit with us?"

"My new friend's are in need of my company right now."

Prince Edward calls to his nephew, "I need a word with you, come over."

"Could it wait 'til after church?"

"Wait here, Suzy." Prince Edward walks over to his nephew and whispers in his ear, "Is there anything wrong?"

"Oh, You thought I was being held against my will. No, uncle, everything is okay and even better than that, these are now our brothers!"

Prince Edward responds with an affirmative, "Yes!"

After Father Marcus assists in the hearing of confessions of the ones who were in need of having their minds cleared of the thoughts that had blocked their hearts, they finally come to rest. The shifting shadows that had kept them from the mercy of God's peace have gone. Now sitting with king Ronan and the others, the Psalms are sung and the scriptures read from the altar of humanity. Father Jim humbly shares a word from the altar at the marriage supper of God as sacrificial, "Lamb."

Father Jim quiets himself before God and begins, "In today's reading on Jesus being tempted in the wilderness, we find the Holy Spirit has come upon Him after being water baptized to fulfill all righteousness as an example for our sakes. Equipped after emptying Himself with a forty day fast on our behalf as well, He is confronted by the devil in three areas of life that we all face. First, being hungry, the flesh of His belly beckons for it to be served by obeying it over God's Holy Spirt with the voice, 'If You are the Son of God, command these stones to be turned to bread.' Jesus denied his flesh and let the Holy Spirit strengthen Him while letting its light address the devil instead with the answer, 'Man doth not live by bread alone.'"

All listen with attentive ears.

"In the second temptation, the evil one then took Him up to the heights and showed Him all the kingdoms of the world in an instant and said, 'All this will be Yours if you bow down and worship me.' You must all remember that Satan wants to keep you in this world and of it. For Jesus answered the devil, 'You shall worship the Lord alone and Him only shall you serve.' God's kingdom of eternal life is not of this world. So, by being born again, your reflection of darkness from this world that you are in needs to be removed. You need the fervent light of God's love 'til you have no more desires to return to what you just came out of. No longer are you to walk in the abuse found in the dark as now your actions should reflect in essence, the Kingdom of His light."

Looking out over the congregation, he pauses to give the people a moment of reflection.

"Finally, you must remember that the demons know scripture as well and they tremble. Be careful that they do not twist them in your mind, for you can wind up wrestling them to your own destruction as the devil spoke to Jesus through God's word, too. Then leading Him to Jerusalem, it made Him stand on the parapet of the temple, and spoke a scripture to Him, 'If you are the Son of God, throw Yourself down from here. For it is written: He will command His angels concerning You, and, with their hands they shall support You lest You dash your foot upon a stone.' Satan tempts Him here as if to say, 'Be proud and take on my being by proving Yourself with man's power in place of God's divine power of humility. Lie to yourself and don't be what God would have You to be in Spirit and in truth. Jesus replied to the prince of darkness, 'It is written, too. You should not put the Lord Your God to the test.' When the devil finished tempting Him with every test, it departed from Him for a time. So walk in the light while there is yet light for you to find a way out and into God's loving arms and you will not be overtaken by evil."

Next after the "Paschal Lamb" is served in the Holy Eucharist to all and while spirits are high, Scorch suddenly stands in the service and testifies, "I have decided to remain by your side, my king. Though first, I must tell you how King Liam died by my own hands."

"How did my father die?"

"A boarlet's blood was painted on the belly of his horse and when its mother was released, it charged and killed him. I was told him by his dying words, "I do not hold my death against you, for as deliverer and king, I know you have been set up by the thoughts that have infiltrated your mind from the evil one"

Captain James becomes enlightened in his thoughts, *"So, that explains it!"*

"You are not that person anymore."

An angry Prince Edward shouts, "My nephew may pardon you, but I do not!"

Ronan stands and faces him, "No greater love doth one have than he lay down his life for a friend."

Scorch becomes saddened, "Yes, he treated me as a friend even though he was dying before me as his enemy. I see now that we are all brothers because we have all been created by the same Father who must be mortified with great grief about his children killing each other."

"Uncle, I would not be standing here without Scorch, for he saved my life."

Prince Edward has a change of heart while rising and begins to smile and testify, "The question now comes, do I trust God or take matters into my own hands? For God is still my God who I still go along with and greatly understand. He has changed my heart from hate to love within as I can no longer kill a brother that I can see myself in."

"King Liam, my father, continues to deliver from the grave, he foreknew that retribution would eventually catch up with these 'Ten.'"

Marcus rises and is insistent, "I will take full responsibility for all of 'The Ten.'"

Prince Edward makes a statement, "Don't you see that it is understood that we are all 'The Ten.' Because of darkness, without guidance from our

Messiah, Jesus the High King, there is no light to see and avoid our sin. For without the truth of Christ, there is no redemption to change our hearts from hate to love to dwell with Him."

"As King, I for one have learned that getting a little too isolated in my comforts can place you out of touch with the way people live their lives. Then growing dim in our vision, we are influenced in our minds while growing cold inside. It is a poor world when love goes missing and mercy dies. For it dries up inside when forgetting how to share while men retreat to be poor."

Eagleheart rises from the crowd and replies as well, "Then we are in agreement that it is the rich who are really poor."

Ronan becomes alert, "A word of caution, truth without compassion is out of season and must ripen on God's vine until it is sweet or we will end up looking down on the people who look down on us."

"Well spoken, my king."

Father Jim looks out over the church from the altar and meets with Prince Edward's and King

Ronan's eyes with an exchange of glances. Edward and Ronan then look at each other as the question comes to mind, who will be king over all, Calington?

Eagleheart looks to Captain James and then to mother, "Won't Ronan be needing our counsel during this situation?"

Rimka answers wisely, "Again, this is a matter of protocol. For this is to be worked out between the members of the royal family and for us to pray to God to have His way so all the voices of the people will be weighed."

Ronan and Prince Edward begin to stare each other down. Fears now rob King Ronan of His joy. He goes to Prince Edward who suspects that he might be after the crown and He in turn feels the same way. Could he want him removed as well?

Realizing the situation they are both in, Ronan yields by calling out to the Prince while walking over to him, "I want to keep the peace in our lands, so I give you authority as King of Eridu to rule, Uncle Edward, as King over all provinces to ensure no blood be spilled."

Prince Edward answers with Ronan now standing before him, but instead in his wisdom, he says, "No. You maintain your rule as king, for I am getting on in years."

Taken by surprise, the king answers, "I have enough to handle on just overseeing Eridu, which almost got overthrown."

"Ronan, I see in you a light that is far above where I was when I was your age. You are the one who is rightly to rule as the youth are our next generation. Do not be afraid, for God is with you. I might be useful as an advisor if you like, but nothing more. Although I am separated from the next generation by age, you'll be more effective in having others identify as our root still holds to the truth for all."

"I never saw it this way before. I suppose I could set Cunna over Eridu as a Lord Protector. Then I could meet with the leader of every province and see how things stand."

"You know the truth that keeps all men's minds free. So, you must guide our new generation as the overseeing king."

"I will pray."

"Continue to stay before the Lord and His mind will remain brilliant within yours. People will see this and follow you for it."

"It is hard to lose sight of His fervent love when He holds my heart so close. He is my strength and source of peace where embracing me with a bond of joy, my vision continually sees."

"My advise is to never lose sight of this fact. For if something doth not look like our Great One and Christ, it is of a dark nature and not within the character of His light.

At the monastery, a release from prayer of intercession is felt. Duff is called to the monsignor's office. He arrives and stands before his desk.

Bartholomew holds up a scroll and hands it to Him, "This is to be delivered to Father Jim in Eridu and he is to read it before the two candidates for king with at least ten witnesses. Your horse is saddled and waiting. Do not stop as I am almost certain that you'll be attacked. So keep your military wits about you with the scriptures you've learned thus far in mind. Do this right away."

Duff stands to attention and salutes Monsignor Bartholomew, "Yes, sir."

"You may go and know that I'll be praying for you."

Out in the courtyard, Duff mounts his horse and sees the gate being opened for him. Once outside, making for the main road, he reaches it and is met by a fierce prevailing wind. A quickening happens within his mind, it is the voice of the monsignor. *"I am almost certain that you'll be attacked."*

Duff responds by speaking out loud, "I can do all things through Christ who strengthens me." A greater wind slows him down from out of the motion of the wind into a stillness that knows even more of the glory of God's presence from within. Another verse comes, bringing more light to mind, *"The fear of the Lord is the beginning of wisdom."*

"Oh! Lord, I am afraid from a lack of understanding all the confusion that I am in. The quiet of Your presence has gone missing in dark clouds once again. Everything is now dim where once your brilliance was within. There is friction in the darkness and the heat of a discomfort that says, *"Go back from where you came. It is much too difficult a journey for you ..."*

"... But now Your heat ignites to flame into a burning light that makes me sane! 'I shall walk in the light as You are in the light that darkness doth not overtake me any longer.'"

"Our days are as a hand breadth ..."

"Yet now Your breath has caught my sail in the stillness of the mighty wind, allowing me to enter back in. There is a gate within Your light where I can breathe eternal life as now though all is dark, I am left without a fright."

"The mind is kept at perfect peace whose mind stays on thee."

"You are my anchor in the storm which takes the place of all that's night. I am guided by Your Spirit through Your door which doth invite."

The winds continue to howl and carry thoughts which hammer at Duff's mind. Yet with each distraction there is a reaction of scripture from his lips 'til these winds of thought die down just past the village of Ostrog as he enters into the mountain pass of Zantee.

The hoofs thrash the ground as he rides hard with the scroll tucked away in his shirt. The Tall Hills come up quick and he is through them twice as fast. For his spirited horse has a breath that seems to ever last. With a cadence not possible to keep except by a Shepard's grace, he is kept as a protected sheep in grazing pastures that are rich and filled with what is alive as now his heart doth thrive. The seeing pools blink when he passes by where next pigs scramble off the road and before he knows it, the road turns off to the entrance of Eridu. Observed by the Calington army, which watches him pass by 'til dust is only seen.

The winded horse starts to slow and seems to know where it doth go. It stops before the church while sounds of praise depart with merry hearts. A gentle breeze meets with Duff who makes his way to its door and enters.

Father Marcus recognizes Duff who is winded from his hard journey, "Corporal, is everything okay?"

"I am looking for Father Jim," he says while catching his breath.

Father Jim opens his eyes from meditating on the Lord and calls out, "I am he!"

Corporal Duff unbuttons his shirt 'til he is able to reach the scroll while walking over to the Father. "This is from Monsignor Bartholomew." He hands it to him.

Jim opens the wax seal as Duff fixes his shirt.

"What doth it say?" asks Duff.

The corporal seems to have asked for everyone. For all eyes are on Jim as he clears his throat to read, "This is a letter from the church archives concerning matters of who shall rule if two members of a family were in conflict. It seems, 'The younger will be assisted by the older as a surrogate King in a transfer of power and this shall preserve peace for a smooth transition for at least a period of two years. For due to the fact that the younger is anticipated to live longer is a wisdom that God has decided within our records.'"

Father Marcus becomes elated and shouts, "This bears witness to what has earlier been decided in confirmation to the truth bearing witness of itself under the guidance of the Holy Spirit of God once again."

Loud shouts of joy come from deep bellicose bellies 'til they work their way through full and lively hearts, "Hal…le…lu…jah!

Everyone is aglow inside a glory cloud of truth, bearing witness of itself in a feast of hugs as God's voice of peace, love, and joy ignites a light that has been established throughout the lands of Calington once again. After so much darkness without any light, the warmth of God's love has thawed every heart and now rules by the truth which welcomes all who have sight. The evil one had people believing that they should try to fit within a dark pit of abuse, but the hatred of its discomfort at last has given way to a home where they belong, the kingdom of The Great One's love.